The TIME Has COME

BROCK BODENSCHATZ

Library of Congress Control Number: 2025924538
ISBN: 978-1-969422-16-4 (Paperback)
       978-1-969422-47-8 (Hardback)
       978-1-969422-17-1 (Ebook)

Olympus Story House
www.olympusstoryhouse.com

1

Wind

The brilliance of the full moon revealed the lone silhouette of a man leaning against the wind, as if he were standing aboard the deck of a ship. As the clouds swept past the moon again he was lost in the shadows created by the trees, their naked branches creaking with each gust of wind. The bluff was high enough above Dering Harbor that the glowing lights of Greenport cast their illumination across the water unmasking the turbulence the wind was creating on the surface. Peter Winthorpe was worried about his boat.

Peter Winthorpe turned his back to the wind. His salt and pepper locks whipped about his face as he returned to the little bed and breakfast he operated with the help of Esmerelda. If the forecasts were right the wind would shift from the east. The harbor would revert to its relative calm during the storm, but something foreboding still haunted his thoughts.

Maybe Esmerelda could tell him what it was. They had been on this quest a long time, been together a long time. He wouldn't have gotten this far without her, but he still had nothing to show for his endurance and was feeling too old to have to start over again.

As he walked back to the house he could already feel the gus·
of wind increasing in strength and magnitude. After years of bein
at sea, he knew this was only the beginning of what would becom
a major storm. At the least, it would delay his pursuit a couple c
days. At most, he might lose his boat and it would end.

"Damn! It's rightfully mine!" He yelled at the night in disgus·
"I'll have it! One way or another." Darkness surrounded him witl
his ideas and notions as he ambled through the night.

The candle lights flickered in accordance with the wind a·
it howled against the window panes of the old house. Esmereld;
continued to shake the bones before spilling them on the tabl·
before her. This world was not presently attached to her thoughts·
but was filled with the chants and rituals from Africa that had been
passed down from mother to daughter for generations. What she
saw in the disarray before her could only be known by a servant
of the true power. Esmerelda was a believer from a long line of
believers and what she saw frightened her. It represented an end to
her existence as she now knew it. As she pondered that fate she was
startled by Peter's appearance in the doorway.

"What is it woman?" he demanded. "I've felt it all night myself.
What did ya see? Tell me!" His patience had grown thin at the
thought of losing what he had searched his whole life for, especially
since he was sure they were so close now.

Esmerelda felt his anguish deep in her soul as if it were her own,
and it was. For the past fifteen years since she had sailed off her
native island of Haiti she had been his companion and confidant.
They have used her powers together in their search, but now as
she fixed her gaze upon the dire look in his eyes, she was afraid to
speak. Afraid of him and for him, afraid for herself and the future.

"I said, tell me woman!" He ordered as he stepped forward
slamming his hand on the table while the bulk of his body hovered
over her.

"Dat be no way of treatin' me, mon, les' you wont a doll full of
pins named afta you!"

Peter didn't appreciate the humor, so she told him what he wanted to know.

"Tree mon be comin'. I tink dey find what we look for."

"Damn! I thought they would have given up after that time in the Yucatan."

"Tis not the same tree." She waited to see his reaction before continuing. There was none. "Da stars bring dem here soon, maybe by da next moon."

"Well, let'em come! We'll be ready for'em!" Peter Winthorpe took confidence in his words. He had fought and won before, and had the scars to prove it. He wasn't going to turn tail and run now. Besides he had Esmerelda and her black magic on his side. Just let them come.

Esmerelda spilled the bones across the black table cloth again, carefully examining their portentous images. The wind shook the old house in its hold on a passing gust as Peter left the room, probably going to draw strength from studying the old log book as he had always done in the past. Esmerelda drew her strength from the darkness like her ancestors before her. The men would come, this was certain, but only Esmerelda knew their destiny. Even VooDoo couldn't change destiny.

The wind blew on.

2

—❦—

Rich Boys

Tyler Martin was a man who had had enough. Enough of anything one could possibly think of. Enough women, booze, travel and other assorted pleasures of various nature. He was ready to reform his evil ways, or so he thought. Money was the foundation to all his adventures. Tyler had the money which gave him the time to indulge in fantasies most men dared not dream of.

From my point of view, I was lucky to meet him when I did. I was living in Key West temporarily on my thirty seven foot sloop, "The Nightwind". After sailing down from Long Island, I was running a day cruise operation using word of mouth advertising to avoid paying taxes on the little income I made. I had only been down there three months and was already two months behind on my dock fees. That's when Jack Rogin blew into town.

Jack Rogin was an old friend, all of the time, and a complete drunk most of the time. His broad shoulders and athletic physique gave him the ominous appearance of a football player. Fact was the pro's wanted him till they found out drinking was his real calling. It didn't bother him though, he didn't want his body all busted up by a bunch of guys that played just for the money. Jack Rogin had lost a fortune, his wife and most of his friends, both distant and close. The Rogin's family estate supported him well enough to keep him out of the labor force. Jack was a remittance man, a character of an extinct breed. He would receive a check monthly provided he never came around to embarrass the family again, as is the case with most remittance men.

I spotted him as he was walking towards my boat.

"What the hell ya doin' down here in the land of the pirates?"

"Looking for a drink, what else," he replied with that big shit eating grin of his.

We shook hands and embraced. It had been more then a few months since the last time I saw Jack. He was good friend and probably one of the nicest guys I ever met. I invited him onboard for a few beers while we shot the breeze.

"So, how'd ya know I was down here?", I asked him after we finished telling each other the usual lies and kicked back with a few beers.

"I didn't till yesterday. I ran into a couple of yuppies who told me they had been out cruising on "The Nightwind". Told me they stuck the captain with a bad check. Thought it was real funny."

"Sonafabitch! I knew it! Never take checks! Shit!"

"Yeah, well, they thought it was real funny till I told them I was your partner. Then they got real serious, said it was all a mistake on their part. Forgot to transfer the money and had overdrawn their account without realizing it, but they would take care of it. The usual bullshit."

"They gave you another check?"

"No way! I told them it had to be cash, you know, to avoid any problems that might occur with our 'records'. They insisted we should have a bonus for any trouble they might have caused, just to show they were sorry about the misunderstanding."

"God damn bastards!"

"Yeah, the phony rich and famous. I told you you shouldn't be hanging out with that type."

"I needed the money. I thought they would be good for it."

"Live and don't learn. That's what I always say."

"I hate to be pushy, but you got it?"

"Sure, I took a little finder's fee for booze, or expenses as you business types call it. Here's the rest."

Jack handed me more money then I had seen in the last three months put together. I had deliberately overcharged these young urban professionals for two reasons. One to pay back what I owed so I could head back to Long Island and two because I hated their phony idea of sophistication and class, like they could buy it with a few extra dollars.

Jack watched as I counted out the money into two separate piles. "What's that for?" he inquired while digging through the ice chest looking for another beer.

"Well, the big pile's for the dock master with a little extra for letting me stay without the hassle. The second's for a night on the town. Whatta ya say?"

"Sure thing, if you don't mind me bringing along a friend. Fact is he'll probably pay for the whole thing. He got more money then my whole family put together, including past generations. He's back at the hotel now, recuperating from the Duval Street crawl."

"What's his name?"

"Tyler Martin. Ever heard of him?"

"No."

"Well, he's in the top twenty richest men in America. Inherited 'a lot' of money a few years back, oil money I think. Anyways, he invested in all the right things at the right time on some info some clerk told him. The clerk heard it from some of those hot shots, the one's that got busted by the SEC, or whatever. Even got called in to testify, but he didn't know nothing, he's just lucky. They let him go. Real nice guy, you'll like him."

"Sounds cool. I need a good night's partying before I sail."

"You headed back to the Island?"

"Yeah, why?"

"I just might have a bidness proposition for ya."

"What ya talking about, Jack? Nothing illegal, I hope. I don't do that kinda shit anymore."

"No, nothing illegal. Let me talk to Tyler about it first, okay? We can talk about it tonight."

"Jack, no offense, but is this guy really cool or are you hanging with him for the free ride?"

"Ya know, that hurts. You probably know me better than anyone, and are probably the only one I know with enough nerve to ask me that." Jack Rogin paused for a moment weighing the words he was about to say carefully. "In the last ten years or so, there've been only two people I've met and trusted as true friends. The kind of friends you'd put your arm in the fire up to here for," indicating his left shoulder with his right hand. "Tyler Martin was one," he paused again showing his embarrassment, "you were the other."

"Thanks, Jack. I appreciate that." I lifted my beer to his and we both sat silently drinking, both feeling estranged yet closer to each other then before.

"So I guess he's okay?" I questioned matter of factly.

Jack eyes opened wide.

"Yeah, he's okay!" After a second we both burst out laughing then uncapped another beer.

Sitting back in the warm tropical air the breeze barely stirred the leaves of the palm trees, but I just had to ask.

"So, what's he worth?"

"Somewhere around a billion." Jack replied without batting an eye.

3

The Bad Guys

Somewhere in the Caribbean, Casper Bennington and his righthand thug, Jim Macy, if that was his real name, were looking for a few good men. Good in the sense that they wouldn't ask questions or defy orders. Casper had a small cargo ship ready to sail on the morning tide and didn't want to be delayed. It had taken almost five years but finally him and Macy knew the port of destination they had been looking for.

Casper Bennington was a man with money made by questionable means. His latest investment was costing him plenty and, as of yet had showed no returns. Him and Macy had been offsetting the costs running drugs and guns, sometimes even human cargo, whatever the occasion called for. Casper was a man with ideas, usually someone else's, but he had the financial backing to carry them out. The problem in the Yucatan cost him plenty but only increased the desire to obtain the unobtainable.

"Doc" Bennington and Macy were literally thrown into a Mexican jail cell to rot after one of their schemes failed and cost two federales their lives. Nine months of bribery yielded little compared to a knife at the base of the skull. They slipped out of the country in the dark of night on an inflatable raft.

As they drifted in the Gulf, Casper swore the treasure would be his no matter what the cost. Macy swore revenge to the man and the witch that caused their trouble. He would get even, he always has. Together they floated for seven days before being spotted and picked up by "Enya"; a cargo ship of unknown origin used for dubious purposes.

Once onboard, Macy pirated the ship for the sole use of "Doc" Bennington's 'expedition'. Macy was a trained killer with little actual history to show for a past. Most believed he was ex CIA, but most also believed he was only loyal to the highest bidder. Right now that was Bennington. "Doc" and Macy watched as the small crew gathered ready to offer their resistance to a hostile takeover. Macy quickly decided who the leader was, walked over and killed him with his bare hands in less then a flash. Just as all hell was about to break loose, Bennington fired a shot into the air.

"The next one who moves gets a bullet! I have enough here for most of you…and as you see, my friend here can take care of the rest!" Casper watched with hidden delight the power the sight of a gun had over men. He waited while they adjusted their attitude to the threat.

"My guess is, you men have one interest…money!" Again he paused to let his words reach their target. "Well…I don't image your lives will change that drastically if you decide to work for me. Of course, if you don't I can't guarantee anything."

The encumbered sound of a dull thud was heard. The men looked on in silent horror as Jim Macy began to hack off bits and pieces of the dead man's body, then began chumming the water along side the ship. The machete was as covered with blood as was his hands as he tossed chunks of flesh into the sea. The sharks had already picked up the scent and were beginning to gather on the port side.

"Well gentlemen, the choice is yours." Casper Bennington turned his back to the men and proceeded to the bridge. Calling over his shoulder, "Make your decisions quickly, we need to make up for lost time!"

The grumbling among the men started to grow till a loud splash was heard and the feeding frenzy began. The crew looked to see Jim Macy standing at the rail covered in blood with the crazed look in his eyes of a deranged man wanting more.

No one decided to fulfill his need.

It was five years later now and most of the original crew was dead. Macy was looking for prospects in The Liar's Saloon on a tiny cay somewhere off another small cay that only the locals knew about. Bennington was standing at the bar in a white sweat stained suit and hat, holding a cane in his left hand. He sipped his drink slowly as the ice melted in the tropical heat. Casper knew one way or the other they would have the men they needed when the ship sailed at dawn; Macy would see to that. What he didn't expect was to be recognized by someone in this third world toilet.

"Doctor Bennington, I presume."

Bennington turned, his face as white with surprise as fear.

"Amanda! What the hell are you doing here?"

"Nice to see you too, Doc. Don't you even offer a lady a drink any more?" Amanda Paige stood inches shy of six foot. She was blonde, lanky and tough, also quite beautiful. She had been through more then most men could endure, but almost always walked away unscathed.

"What are you doing here?" Doc was visibly agitated.

"I'm studying medicine at the local college. I want to be a doctor just like you!" The irony in her voice wasn't lost in it's increasing volume. "What the hell do you think I'm doing!? I've been island hopping back to the States ever since you deserted me back in South America!" Time hadn't healed the wound and it was obvious.

"Sorry, Amanda. It couldn't be helped. They would have killed us if they caught us. We had to leave when we did. You can understand that, can't you?" Bennington was trying hard to win her over again, all the time knowing it was impossible with her type.

"You could have sent for me."

"I couldn't take the chance. That might have led them right to us." Doc searched the room for Macy, he was anxious to depart. He was sure he knew where this was leading, though rather surprised by the next statement.

"Well…don't fret honey. I was just busting your chops." She smiled for the first time and it was definitely apparent the years were taking their toll. "Listen, I heard you and Macy were killed in Mexico, chasing a treasure that wasn't even there."

Uncomfortably, Bennington continued the conversation. "It wasn't exactly like that, really. We did run into some trouble though."

"Well, I had my fortune told me by some VooDoo queen, I don't remember her name, but she told me all about it. She even told me we would meet again, and we did, didn't we? Weird, huh?"

"Where did you meet this woman?" Anxiety and alarm were more then obvious in Bennington's voice, even to Amanda who had been drinking at a steady pace all evening.

"I'm not sure, really. It was a few islands ago and a long time." Amanda started to feel the loss of control in herself and attributed it to the liquor. Even Doc Bennington hadn't seen Macy fill half her glass with a slow poison. As Amanda laid her head on the table, Casper Bennington headed for the door. He knew Macy would be on board with a crew when it was time to leave, there was no use him losing sleep over it.

4

❦

Night Out

*J*ack Rogin and Tyler Martin were sitting at the bar of Kyushu's when I arrived. They had either been somewhere else before hand or had arrived extremely early. Then again, knowing Jack, he probably just continued to party since he had left my boat that afternoon. Anyway, it was obvious that Tyler Martin had given up on his idea to reform, at least temporarily.

Damn, I hated playing catch up.

Jack introduced me to Tyler and right away we hit it off. Jack was right, Tyler was a regular kind of guy, without pretense or any illusion. In fact, the only thing that bothered me about him was his constant referring to me as 'old boy' or to me and Jack as 'old chaps', but he even that he managed to explain away.

"I'm sorry, old boy, can't help it, old habit. I was raised by an old English nanny. Very proper." He mimicked with an extended pinky. "I never knew there were other ways to speak till I was a teenage. Slang came first, I suppose. Then languages. French first, then Spanish and Italian. Then I rebelled and wanted to learn Japanese. My parents thought I was crazy, so I worked extra hard at it." He paused suddenly, as if the thought of something he said had grabbed him. "I'm sorry, I've lost the point, haven't I, old boy? Which was the point, wasn't it?"

We had all lost the point and were glad when Tyler suggested we go in to get some dinner.

More saki with dinner brought about more lost points in a conversation that included the philosophies of life and death, the faults and troubles with religion and who was funnier Bugs Bunny or Daffy Duck. That one we left hanging, depending on who the co star was.

All and all, it was turning out to be one helluva goodtime. Our little shoji room was the busiest place on the island, between waitresses coming in and out with saki and sushi, the passing patrons Jack and Tyler kept pulling in for a drink, I figured I was back in debt to someone. When the check came Tyler picked up the whole tab including a hundred dollar tip for each and every waitress, cook and bartender in the place.

"Thanks again, Tyler," I repeated when we hit the street. "I really do appreciate your generosity."

"Don't even think about it, old boy. Fact is, I probably made more money in interest alone during the time we spent in there. Besides, that was the best sushi I ever had, even better then in Japan."

"You've been to Japan too?"

"He's been everywhere, haven't ya Tyler? He's even been to Cuba." Jack said pointing ninety miles south as he rejoined our party after calling a cab to take us down to The Bull on Duval Street.

"No shit. How'd you manage that?" I had to ask having always wanted to go myself.

"I bought a bogus passport in Mexico. It almost backfired on me though. It seems the name on the passport was the same as an old friend of Fidel's. He actually came to see me at the hotel. When he found out that I was much too young to be the man he thought I was, he apologized profusely for disturbing me before leaving. The whole time he had a smile on his face. I took the warning. I was out of there before any other complications."

After the taxi made its way through the mopeds, bicycles and other various tourist congestion along Duval it dropped us off across the street from The Bull. Key West wasn't what it was ten or fifteen years ago. Commercialism had come into town in a big way, covering up what had originally been its main attraction, seclusion. The end of the road. Next stop the third world. Hopefully, in another ten or fifteen years things would fade away and come full circle, back to what it used to be, a remote little town at the outskirts of America.

We didn't stay long at The Bull, too many other bars to stop at and the night was growing small. A drink here, a drink there, that's the way it is in this town. Stay in one spot too long you've either passed out or dead.

"Hey, why aren't we goin' in here?" Jack called out to Tyler and myself who were a few steps ahead of him.

"You don't wanna go in there, Jack. Nothin' but college jocks. We'll end up with puke all over our shoes." But I could see there was no talking him out of it. He had vowed to stop at every bar we passed and he wasn't going to break that vow now.

"I guess we're going in, old boy." Tyler responded as we turned and headed back to the door.

A second before we would have entered the bar a girl of not more than nineteen ran out the door directly into Tyler. They both mumbled "Sorry", to each other just as a large looking jock grabbed her arm from behind.

"Where the hell you think you're goin'?" the jock rambled trying to maintain his balance while she struggled to free herself.

"I told you to keep your fuckin' hands off me!" but the jock still had his grip on her.

"Listen, I've been buying you drinks…"

Tyler Martin took hold of the jock's gripping hand and twisted his thumb back. With a look of deep pain on his face he released the girl. Jack pushed me and the girl to the side as Mr. Macho in all his beer inflated ego came face to face with Tyler Martin.

"You oughta mind your own business, asshole!"

Tyler didn't flinch. The good ol' boy's friends were starting to gather around the doorway, waiting to see their hero tear the little guy apart. I was getting a little worried till Jack said to me, "You're gonna love this."

The big guy took three swings at Tyler and with only the slightest of movements Tyler ducked all three potential blows. Then he yawned in the jock's face which of course angered and frustrated him even more. He charged at Tyler who stepped aside. With two fingers to the man's back and two fingers to the man's forehead, he sent him flipping onto his back in the street. It was the best display of aikido I had ever seen. As expected, this display drew out more of the fallen boy's friends onto the sidewalk to avenge his less than heroic landing.

Tyler was throwing them in all directions without any real damage to any of them other then their pride. More then half the football team was scattered on the street in less then a minute's time. Jack was laughing his ass off while the girl stood there shocked by the whole scene. Then some of the boys started getting up again and were grabbing anything they could to use for weapons. When I heard the bottle shatter and the saw the jagged edge of glass I stepped in front of the man in his attempt to get to Tyler. In his frenzy for revenge he slashed wildly at me with the broken end of the bottle.

Big mistake, before either of us even realized it I had broken his arm by instinctive reaction, then leveled two more attackers with a couple roundhouse kicks into a jumping front kick. This time they didn't get up.

"Tyler, it's time to end the party! We gotta go!" Jack had already put the girl in a cab as Tyler and I finished downing any further attackers. While we moved away police sirens could be heard coming closer.

Pointing Tyler into the bar, I waved Jack on and entered the door. Even with all the people who streamed out to see what was happening the bar was still crowded. We switched jackets then quickly altered our appearances while moving through the throng of people: a changed part of the hair, no tie where there once was one, glasses, no glasses. We left the bar two minutes later unrecognized by the victims, the witnesses or the police.

"I guess Jack got away alright." Tyler remarked as we sauntered down Duval.

"Provided he didn't hurt himself laughing."

"Where do you suppose he went?"

"Probably back to your hotel, I guess."

"I doubt it. They threw us out this afternoon."

"What?"

"Well, actually they asked us to leave very politely. After I offered to pay for all the complaint's rooms, but since the island is booked right now, there was no where else for them to go. So, we left. Jack said he would make us other arrangements. I don't know."

The heat in the tropical night air was making my head ache as the dreaded 'saki hangover' began to fill the base of my skull with its unique distinctive pain.

"I know where he is. We better pick up some beer. There's none left."

5

The Deluge

Peter Winthorpe admitted to himself he never thought of pirates as being in a cold climate. Sun tanned bodies working the riggings as light winds blew across the water. His years at sea had changed that image drastically. He felt winter's chill in the wind as it cut into his being while trying to remove the fallen tree the continuing storm had produced. His only comfort was knowing his boat was safe. The wind had shifted.

Trouble had always followed Peter Winthorpe, or so it seemed. His life began abruptly with the death of his mother when he was five. His father was a seaman aboard any ship he could work. Peter's world became the sea as his father brought him along. His only knowledge was of ships, charts and navigation, and that alone made him cleverer than his old man. Peter's father worked but never learned. He died when Peter was twelve.

The only possession his father left him were the old log books from his great ancestor who sailed as a pirate. They were said to point to a treasure to the one who could read them, as the family folklore said. How they had escaped being lost in the shipwreck was a mystery on its own. Peter believed the boat had recently visited its homeport before the wreck and was left with family or friends, perhaps his ancestor had a vision as to his fate. Peter now believed that home port to be Sag Harbor.

The storm still raged in its growing fury as the chain saw ripped through the branches of the fallen tree. Wind swept the rain so that it hurt the skin on contact. Peter was piling the cut limbs when he was startled by the sight of Esmerelda standing in the rage of the storm.

"Peta, we must leave here berry soon!" The look of terror in her eyes went totally unnoticed by Peter Winthorpe.

"What are ya daft, woman. We ain't goin' nowhere." His look was as wild as hers, but their reasons were different. He wasn't giving up, but her reason was deeper. Fear had entered her heart as it never had done before.

"Peta, listen to me. We must go. Hide, somewhere."

"Whatta yer talkin' 'bout?" He approached her with an air to intimidate her but right away saw it was useless. Her fear was real and deep, unlike anything he had witnessed to date.

"Peta, you don't undarstand. The mon from Mexico, they come again."

"You said it was different men!"

"Jes! Dey come too, Tree mon. Dey all come, Mexico mon too."

"So let'em come. Let'em all come!"

"No! De bad mon from Mexico, ju know da one. He know da magic now too. A new one come wit dem. He know too. Berry strong. Berry, berry strong."

Peter Winthorpe's mind raced as the cold sweat turned his body wet and sent a shiver up his spine. His face was white with fear but he was even more determined not to give up. He had seen the coldblooded slaughter at the hand of the doctor's men. Many men had died that day and it was all so senseless. Peter's treasure wasn't in Mexico, he knew that, he just didn't know where it was. It was just another point of reference on the route to him. One that led him from Rio through the Caribbean to the Yucatan Peninsula, on that particular day.

Esmerelda had shown him the way through guidance and magic. She knew the islands and their culture, how to read signs that had been lost through the course of time passed. He knew the terms of the sea, even the old terms no longer used, and the tides that would carry a ship from one port to the next. Together, but only together, they could find and lay claim to Winthorpe's treasure. They both knew it was close though neither could pinpoint the location. Both were looking in their own way. Too many years had passed and now they were both afraid more time would only bring failure.

The storm blew its wind and rain and cold fury before it, but Peter could only see the past. And now he was afraid his past would be his only treasure with its hopes and dreams unfulfilled. A lifetime of searching for nothing more than a dream.

"Peta, Peta!" Esmerelda could see there was no talking to him now. He had immersed himself into his world of schemes and plots with more dreams of fortune at its end. He continued at the task at hand of piling more branches on the stack, but the blank look on his face had changed little.

Esmerelda returned to the shelter of the house. It was rare that the little bed and breakfast had guests during the middle of the week, especially long before the usual summer season began. A young couple had checked in before the storm hit and the woman was understandably startled by the crashing of a tree against the house so close to their window. Esmerelda was about to knock on the door to tell them everything was alright when she heard the rattling of the old brass bed and the low moans. Apparently, the woman had other things on her mind now. Esmerelda smiled as on tip toe she left down the hallway. The sound of the chain saw from out in the storm brought Peter to the fore front of her mind.

"Dat mon es goin' to need sumting berry good tonight." She thought to herself and quickly went off to make the preparations.

6

Amanda

The drone of the diesels was all that could be heard at that moment in the small storage cabin next to the engine room. The cargo ship had left on the tide as planned with the needed crew and one extra. The boat was on the open ocean now, headed for points unknown in a northerly direction. The exact destination was known only by "Doc" Bennington and that bothered Macy. Up until now he had been privy to every detail, but "Doc" now would only tell him Long Island. He said that when Amanda had shown up he was fearful that others from their past might follow, at least that was how he put it to Macy. It would be safer if only he knew where they were headed. Macy knew seeing Amanda again had really shaken Bennington up.

Amanda Paige was the typical story of a good girl who lost her way, well maybe not exactly. She had come down to Rio de Janeiro with some college friends for Mardi Gras but never went back. During her vacation stay she learned of the death of both her parents in a car crash somewhere on Interstate 80. Something in her brain snapped and the budding career as a lawyer was swept away, as was anything else that held the past in its grip. A new life as barmaid, waitress and even hooker paid the way for life below the equator.

For a while the diversion worked, but when the years started to add up she felt the pull to go home again. She had grown up an only child and was use to the feeling of being alone. She didn't mind it but in the States she felt at home, here it was just a party that could never convey any real sense of emotion to her. Now it was time to go back. The emotions that she had escaped she now needed, only now she didn't have the means to return. She had no regrets, she just needed a ticket.

That's when her luck changed, not particularity for the better. One night two high rollers came into the bar, Americans. Casper Bennington fell head over heels at the first sight of Amanda Paige. "Doc" and Macy had been plundering villages to the north and came to Rio to party before leaving Brazil. Macy didn't like seeing Bennington shower the girl in the wealth they had pillaged. The local police eventually weren't to happy about it either.

Amanda saw "Doc" Bennington as her ticket home and he probably would have done anything to take her with him too. What neither of them counted on was another stranger in town. Another player with an appetite to party. Said to be from a very wealthy American family. Amanda couldn't help but fall in love with his easygoing nature and athletic stature.

The man might have been a fly in the ointment to Bennington but he was just the dupe Jim Macy was looking for. Macy knew the federales were getting closer to the ancient treasures him and "Doc" had looted, he could smell them. This guy was the perfect stooge in Macy's eyes; he could set him up for the fall and break up Bennington's little romance at the same time. Not that he didn't think Amanda was a looker, but babes always brought trouble when it came to business.

Macy's only mistake was trying to get Jack Rogin drunk enough to use him in his plan. Jim Macy might have been an expert at weapons, explosives, torture and various forms of death, but when it came to drinking Jack Rogin had no match. If it wasn't for Casper

Bennington Macy would have ended up in a Brazilian prison. They made it out of the country just in time. Bennington left his prize Amanda behind, for even to him the prize of gold was much more important.

The Government Bureau of Antiquities had no evidence that Jack had been involved in any of the theft of their historic pieces. They quietly asked him to leave the country, which at this time he was more then happy to comply with. The only one who was left empty handed was Amanda. Well, not exactly, she had been selling the baubles "Doc" was giving her on the black market all along. She brought a ticket for Trinidad and was out of the country even before Jack Rogin.

The trip home was taken at her own pace. If she liked an island she stayed for a while. If she didn't, she'd make some money and leave for the next island. That's the way it was when her path crossed Bennington's and Macy's again.

Now Macy's face showed the contortions of a man possessed. The boom of the ships engines along with the tape of the Petro drums blaring from the ghetto box in the corner set the mood. The loa had mounted Macy upon his passing Legba at the gate. The flesh of the body before him was painted with the signs of deities to come. Candles illuminated the cabin as it swayed on the open sea with its fragrant scents mixed amongst the aromas of potions, blood, diesel and clairin. Her soul was gone, but the body would return for what ever purpose Macy intended for it. Dead, yet not dead. Living, yet not living. Amanda Paige was going home.

Casper Bennington had been sleeping until the ship started to move out of the harbor. He stared out his porthole at what he knew would be the last sight of land for some time. He hated being at sea. If it wasn't for the men's fear of Macy, he knew he wouldn't be able to maintain control of a ship at sea. He knew nothing about ships, charts or navigation. He usually spent the first week in his cabin driving the porcelain bus, but now even as the ship had entered the open sea, "Doc" could barely hear the haunting screams that seemed to echo through his mind, distance, yet too close to dismiss. This anxiety saved him from the usual seasickness but left him with an empty need that wouldn't let him rest. He thought he could hear the sound of drums and they were pounding away at his brain.

Casper was beginning to feel paranoia in its deepest sense. Between the killings and now Macy's obsession with the occult, or whatever it was, Casper felt he was being manipulated. That was the main reason "Doc" didn't tell Macy the details of their journey. This would be the longest leg of their campaign. "Doc" knew he needed Macy but he thought he had let him run wild too long. Now he was going to try to 'domesticate' an animal that probably couldn't even spell the word.

Bennington even thought Amanda showing up when she did was no coincidence. He had figured she was in some banana republic jail all this time.

"Doc" paced the floor of his cabin wondering what to do with Macy when he realized the sounds in his head were coming from the ship. Sticking his small caliber pistol in his suit jacket pocket, he began to roam the lower corridors in search of their origin. The men who saw him retreated quickly wanting to remain anonymous and alive, but Bennington was only searching for the persecuting sound that visited his mind and drove him on to where his fears didn't want him to go. The drums growing louder all the time as the heat from the engines increased in the companionway as he moved forward.

"Doc" Bennington stood before the door as the sweat began to trickle down his face and stained his open collar. He pulled the pistol from his pocket and prepared himself for a sight he could have never prepared for. Instantly swinging the door open, he saw a nude Macy cut the throat of a chicken, while in his frenzied dance let the blood splatter over himself and the naked figure on the floor. The scene frightened and appalled Bennington, he stepped back from the door still bewitched to watch. He saw the vevers drawn on the floor and realized the nature of Macy's actions. Voodoo. His eyes were attracted to the body which was at the center of the room when a spasm caused it to stir. Then all at once the drums stopped and Bennington realized it was Amanda Paige. Macy was standing over her exposed flesh with the dead chicken in one hand and the knife in the other. The maniacal grin on his face caused a shiver to run down Bennington's back before he broke out in a cold sweat.

"What the hell's she doing here?" "Doc" babbled out while trying to regain a composure of authority.

Macy stood leering forward not quite able to focus on any one point. His head turned as he twisted his neck as if trying to remove a kink from it, then returned his stare forward, otherwise motionless. His expression remained the same.

A feeling of nausea overcame Bennington and he retreated down the companionway with no particular destination. Slowly the body of Amanda Paige began to rock on the floor to the rhythm of the engines. Macy had accomplished his miracle. He had felt its power as his mind rejoined the world of faxes and cellular phones.

"Doc" Bennington stood at the ship's railing. He had suddenly developed a new love of the ocean in its simplest calling. Clear sky and blue water, what else was important in life. The sea was the origin of life itself and the realization of life, his life, was his most vital concern at that moment. Macy was out of his control, he knew it and he was afraid Macy knew it too. Bennington knew that they still needed each other, he could only hope that Macy was still within reason to see it also.

Bennington looked across the placid water, thinking, then hurled every bit of substance in his stomach into the sea.

7

❧

Heroes

"Well, he's not here!"

"No sign of him, old boy?"

"Not that I can tell." I came up from below deck. "Either he's still with the girl or he found an open bar somewhere."

"My guess is a bar."

"Mine too." I took a quick look around the boat, everything seemed all right. "Well, there's a little place on the other side of the marina. Locals hangout there, no tourists usually. I don't think the place even has a name."

"When he came back to the hotel, he was talking about a place with no walls, just a deck overhead."

"That's the place."

We walked around the marina with a growing feeling of elation as the sound of Jack's voice carried on the still night air. Neither Tyler nor myself had expressed the idea openly that maybe Jack hadn't been so lucky and was picked up by the police, though we both had thought about it. The euphoria became a sinking feeling of doom upon hearing his topic of discussion.

"Hail the conquering heroes! Here they are now!" Jack shouted across the bar. "The two men who single handedly, or is it double handedly, whatever, defeated the entire Northern State football team."

As we stepped into the dim lights of the bar we received a hardy round of applause from the few remaining patrons.

"Jack, what are you doing?" Tyler grabbed Jack by the arm and shook him.

"Watta ya mean? I'm making you guys into heroes. Local legends."

Jack had that big dopey grin of his smiling right at Tyler, and while Tyler was getting nervous that someone might tip the cops to our whereabouts, he couldn't help but smile back. Meanwhile I was scanning the cast of characters sitting at the bar. Two of them I knew did a little smuggling to supplement their incomes, the other had run away from his wife and her charge accounts, the rest were friends of one or the other.

"Hi guys." I knew most of them by sight and they knew me maybe a little less. Aside to Tyler I said, "Don't worry, they're okay," just loud enough that they might hear and feel honored by our trust.

Lorraine was working the bar that night as she does six of the seven nights of the week. Lorraine had been born in Brooklyn but grew up in Bermuda. She seemed to spend her life constantly sliding down the globe south. That was how she had, so far, ended up in Key West. Not that it was hard to do, but she could always pick out the tourists who happen to come into the bar. Usually they left after one drink, but Jack Rogin had spent the whole afternoon without spending more then a large tip. Lorraine had eased him into the evening crowd which tends to be a bit rough with outsiders.

Now, as we stood at the bar ordering drinks for all, she began to ask about our adventures of the evening, which now seemed so long ago.

"There's really not much to tell." Tyler offered with a chuckle from the other end of the bar. "They didn't want to be sociable." That brought a full fledged roar of laughter as all listened.

Lorraine began to talk to me on the side. "Those guys really had it coming. They'd been tearing up the town the last three days." She paused while filling my glass with what was left in the shaker. "The local team was beaten by Northern State, they came down just to rub it in, I guess. They lost in the finals. Probably needed an ego boost."

"How sporting." I sarcastically replied. I was never a big fan of jocks and their attitude anyway. "Let's rub it in a little more."

"It may have started out that way, but then they started to get destructive. After that, beating up the locals became the major past time."

"Hail the conquering heroes." I mockingly retorted.

"You guys were just doing a public service." Jack burst in. "The unsung heroes of the modern world."

"The island telegraph had the news here even before Jack." Lorraine added to regain my attention. "You boys really did make an impression."

"That's what we're afraid of." Tyler threw in after appeasing the local curiosity of the sordid details.

"I was hoping to set sail for the homelands tomorrow."

"You're leaving us?" Lorraine questioned with the very slightest hint of a sob and surprise in her voice.

"Have to. Not enough money to stay here all year."

"We might be able to work something out there." Tyler butted in. By now, everyone was feeling the effects of the evening's binge over the line, except maybe Jack who quickly continued Tyler's line of thought.

"That's right. I wanted to talk to you about that." As if suddenly remembering his task for the evening. "You're sailing tomorrow. That's perfect. We need a place to stay."

I looked at Tyler and we both started to laugh.

"I've heard rumor to that effect."

Tyler offered Lorraine five hundred bucks for a case of rum and two cases of Coronas, but she would only take the cost of the rum. The beer was a going away present provided we came back next year. We promised that was a sure thing. Three cases were all we could carry anyway, even that was a problem with the swaggering along the narrow walkway to my boat.

"You plan on leaving right away?" Jack was compelled to question as we loaded the booze on board.

"No, I think we better get some food first." I'm sure the sarcasm was lost on Jack. "Besides, don't you guys have luggage?"

"The hotel said they would hold it till we sent for it. Are we all going to fit on here?" Tyler's concern was appreciated.

"It'll be tight, but we can manage it." The "Nightwind" could sleep four comfortably, it wouldn't be any problem with three on board. "We'll have to stay close to the coast and put in most of the time, though. We can't carry enough supplies and water for more then a day or two."

"That's fine with me."

"Me too!" Jack added in all seriousness.

The eastern skies had already began to show the light of morning on the horizon, it was slight but it was there. I was looking over the "Nightwind" under the scrutiny of Jack and Tyler.

"Gentlemen, barring any unforeseen circumstances, we'll set sail on the evening tide. I suggest you get some rest. Tomorrow will be a busy day."

8

⋆

Night of Madness

Esmerelda looked herself over in the mirror. She wasn't in too bad a shape for a woman her age, even if she did say so herself. A little overweight maybe, but her body was firm and her skin smooth. She was humming a chant her mother had taught her many years ago as she ground the pestle into the herb filled mortar. She was nude, for nudity added to the purity of heart which was needed to create the potion she desired. Some would call it an aphrodisiac, others a love potion, but to Esmerelda it was just a little bit of magic stimuli used to help create another 'night of madness'.

The room at the other end of the house, away from the guest's rooms, was lit with numerous candles. The bed had been turned down though she wasn't sure if they would actually use it. Sex toys of all varieties were spread out on top of the bureau for what ever the occasion called for. The handcuffs had always been her favor for some reason. She had continually been surprised by Peter's willingness to be subdued in this manner since he had a grave fear of confinement, but it gave her the power to prolong the passion at her own slow pace.

Earlier, Esmerelda bathed in a tub of scented oils. Now that the potion was a powdery talc, she took a portion and mixed it with scented body oils, rubbing it into assorted parts of her body's erogenous zones. She took the remaining potion and stirred it into a kettle of hot water and rum, making a brew for herself and Peter to imbibe at the stroke of midnight. As the hour approached, she began to decorate her body with jewelry and other objects of enchantment and culture from her past.

Peter Winthorpe sat in the tower of the house studying the old log book and looking at the charts. Occasionally he raised his eyes to look out over the water as the storm continued to blow. The tower had been added onto the house over a hundred and fifty years before, back when Sag Harbor was in its heyday as a whaling port. In those days you had a three hundred and sixty degree view of the waters surrounding Shelter Island. The whaling ships could be spotted rounding the north end of Gardiners Island, giving the families on Shelter Island time to get to Sag Harbor before the boats reached port. Now though, a few trees on the high side of the island partially blocked the view.

Peter put down the book and rubbed his eyes. It was close to midnight and Esmerelda had asked him to be down before then. He knew she was up to something, he could smell the candles even up in the tower. The smell reminded him of a night years ago when they had just bought the old house. Esmerelda had been taking him through the blissful stages of sex and magic when there was a knock on the door. It was unusual for a guest to come to this side of the house especially after midnight. Peter had thrown on a robe and answered the door.

"Yes, can I help you?" Before him stood a beautiful Mexican woman who was spending the weekend alone. She was of medium height with exquisite waist long black hair and big brown eyes. The silk robe she wore allowed her harden nipples to protrude against the soft material showing off her shapely figure.

"I'm sorry to intrude, but the scent of sex is making me crazy! Would you mind if I joined you?"

Peter stood at the doorway with his mouth agape. The heat in his loins the moment he saw this vivacious temptress entering the house now turned to fire. He turned to Esmerelda somewhat embarrassed, he didn't know what to say. Esmerelda stood there in black leather boots to her thighs with five inch heels holding a cat o nine tails slung back over her shoulder. She stared at Peter then smiled.

"Well, don't keep da lady waytin'."

The menage a trois lasted well into the next evening. The various partners, voyeurs, positions, daisy chains, toys and magic left them all exhausted. When Maria left there was no charge. She never returned, but Peter and Esmerelda still spiced their love sessions with talk of her as if she were there.

Peter sat back remembering. He rubbed his eyes again and looked out towards Gardiners Island, then to Sag Harbor, then back again. He didn't expect to see a face looking back at him.

Scared, he pushed back against the chair and fell, but never took his eyes off the image in the glass. Its ghostly face had a patch over its left eye and an odd looking hat on its head. It faded from sight when Esmerelda yelled up the tower stairs.

"Petar! Where you at, mon? It be time."

"I'll be right down!" He yelled with more then a hint of agitation in his voice. He picked himself up and looked at the glass but all he saw was the bay beyond.

Making his way down the winding stairway, he was sweaty and pale when he emerged into the lower hallway. Esmerelda was standing at the bedroom doorway waiting when she saw the frighten look on his face.

"What be da matta wit you. You look like you see a ghost or sometin'."

"I fell asleep, you startled me. I was havin' a bad dream." He ran his fingers through his salt and pepper hair and shook his head back.

"Well dreamin' time is over. Dis gonna be da real ting." She grabbed him by the shirt pulling him into the room and closed the door.

9

Zombie

A thousand miles away, Jim Macy was pounding his flesh into Amanda Paige. Her motionless body took each stroke as he forced himself harder and harder till he finally came. She was aware of what was happening, she had taken enough drugs and alcohol that a few more burnt brain cells from whatever poison wasn't going to have that much effect on her unless it killed her. She thought once the nausea left her stomach she could better evaluate her situation and what to do about it.

Macy left when he was done. The stuffy cabin next to the engine room was hot, it made her headache even worse. Macy had washed her down after his little dance routine but she was desperately wanting to take a shower. She was glad she had had her tubes tied long ago when she was in Rio. She didn't want to be producing anymore bastards like Macy into this world. She was wearing nothing but a dog collar that Macy had put around her neck but that wouldn't stop her if she saw the chance to escape.

Amanda knew she was on the open sea by the way the boat rolled on the swells. Things didn't look good, but at least she was alive even if she did feel like she was visiting hell. Her chance would come, like it always had. Maybe they wouldn't always go the way you wanted but they changed the course of things, and that was what was important. Playing zombie for now would keep her alive till that chance came.

"No body, no questions, right? And it wasn't like she was there long enough for any one to miss her, right? She's just a whore, who cares?"

Macy had come up from the bowels of the ship after his death dance and pleasures to the sunlight of the upper deck. He had showered and wiped away his war paint. Now he was preoccupied trying to figure out what was running through the mind of Casper Bennington.

"Doc" Bennington stood at the rail of the "Enya" looking out to sea. In his left hand was the bottle of rum he was using to wash the taste of vomit out of his mouth and dull his nerves. The silence that hung in the air with a sense of authority between them was definitely in Bennington's favor.

"So, what do you plan to do with her?" Casper asked with a controlled voice.

Macy looked at him nervously. Whatever he had in mind was stripped from his conscious at that moment. Bennington smiled and laughed.

"Keep her if you want! Just keep her outta my sight, okay."

Bennington laughed again, then headed up to the wheel house to check on their position. The sweat that was dripping from his body staining his clothes even more then usually was the only sign of the real fear he had of Macy. Apparently he still had some control over him he thought. The gun he held in his right hand had given him the courage he needed, but perhaps witnessing Macy's black magic also fostered a new strength within himself.

Macy stood at the rail trembling. He saw his advantage fall like raindrops in the ocean. He saw the change in Bennington and knew it meant a new balance of power had been created between them. He wanted nothing more than to kill Bennington, but he still needed him for now. It took all the control he could muster not to rip Casper's throat out.

"If he really thought that pop gun in his pocket saved him," Macy shook his head as he thought to himself. "Let him think what he wants, when the time comes what he thinks won't matter any way. If this treasure hunt we're on yields half of what it's supposed to, I won't need anybody ever again."

Macy retreated into the ship, his time would come but not soon enough, and definitely not yet. Now it was time to visit his little play thing.

The man at the ship's wheel was only a boy of nineteen, perhaps. The dreadlocks on his head and cigar size joint that hung from his lip hid the fact that his father was a Jamaican police chief. Sheraton Quinn had run away from home a long time ago. He had been working on ships for more then half his life. He had been all through the Caribbean, South America and Mexico. Now he was headed to someplace in America called Long Island. He thought maybe he would stay there if he liked it. Bennington and Macy didn't scare him, he had seen them all come and go. Tough guys were too intense to keep it up forever. They either got themselves killed or burnt out and quit. It didn't matter to Sheraton. His life was a constant flow with the tides, but he was a bit startled to see Bennington enter the wheelhouse for the first time since he took control of the ship.

"And what can I do fo' you, Mistar Bennington?"

"First, you can put that shit out. The smell makes me sick."

"No problem, mon." Sheraton took the joint from his mouth, rolled the burning herb on his wet lips to extinguish it, then placed it back in his mouth for later use.

"I want you to show me where we are." Bennington walked over to the chart table. Sheraton set the wheel into its makeshift autopilot to join him at the table.

"I be guessin' we be right about dere." He pointed after a few seconds of perusing the chart.

"Can't you be a little more sure then that?" Bennington was more then slightly annoyed by the less then conclusive response.

"Not on dis boat, mon. Got no way of knowin' wiffout seein'."

"Don't you have radar or something?" Bennington was visibly agitated as his voice rose.

"All dis boat has is dat radio and it don't always work." Sheraton pointed by nodding his head towards the small VHF sitting in the corner to the left of the chart table. He left Bennington looking at the chart and returned to steering the ship. He checked his bearing on the compass and made the slight adjustment needed.

Bennington stood staring at the chart.

"This shouldn't be too hard to figure out." He mumbled to himself.

After a while, Bennington came away from the table. He was sure he understood it now and was quite pleased with himself. He was watching Sheraton at the wheel, in a somewhat absent minded manner, wondering to what advantage he could use his new found knowledge. "Doc" noticed he still held the bottle of rum in his left hand, he offered it to Sheraton.

"Like some?"

"No, tanks, mon. I don't be a drinkin' mon." Sheraton was eyeing Bennington curiously. What was he up to?

"Just what is it dat you be lookin' fo, Mistar Bennington?"

Bennington gazed out from the bridge, there was nothing to see but open ocean and blue skies with the occasional large white puffy clouds that looked like cotton suspended in the air. His mind drifted back to years ago. Everything seemed so sure then, like clouds in a blue sky, but as his life passed through time the clouds seemed to close in. Nothing was clear anymore. Nothing was separate onto itself. His eyes tried to fix themselves on the horizon where blue sky met blue water, but they couldn't. He shook his head and muttered to himself, "I'm getting to old for this shit." He took a swig of rum and placed his attention on Sheraton.

"When you get a better fix on our position, come to my cabin and tell me. I'll probably be there the rest of the day."

Bennington left the wheelhouse and headed right to his cabin. He needed time to think. A plan was needed. In fact, two plans were needed.

Bennington was beginning to realize that going into American waters wasn't going to be as easy as hopping around the third world. He hoped this damned treasure was going to be worth it. He felt it was time to retire, get that villa he always wanted, a swimming pool with beautiful girls to wait on him everyday. It wouldn't be Mexico though, not anymore, or South America. Maybe somewhere in Africa or Indonesia. Somewhere the locals never heard of him or didn't care if they did.

In what amounted to a direct conscious effort, Bennington remembered what the main reason for this expedition was in the first place.

Revenge.

Macy and him had sat in a Mexican cell battling rats and roaches for space, all because they were in the wrong business when they accidentally ran into the local federales. Bennington was sure they had been set up. The Brit and the witch doctor got away, but they wouldn't get away next time. Their time to pay was coming.

"Damn! I really am getting too old for this. How could I have forgot that?" "Doc" was talking aloud to himself as he paced the floor of his cabin. He took another swig of the rum he still held and stared out the porthole. He could see the stacks of an ocean liner just over the horizon.

"Damn tourists! They're making this world too damn small!" He sat back on his bunk against the wall, thinking about the past , present and future of "Doc" Casper Bennington.

———————

The rusted red ship cut through the water on its way north to the new world. Changes were coming, everyone on board knew it. This ship had never been north of the Bahamas before and the crew had an uneasy feeling it wasn't going to see the south side of them again. Everyone onboard was thinking of their options as Sheraton Quinn kept the "Enya" pointed to the promised land as marijuana smoke filled the bridge.

10

❦

A Face I Can't Forget

The cold spray of the harbor smacked off the bow of the dinghy hitting Peter Winthorpe directly in the face, it was the only place the foul weather gear didn't cover. Its bitter cold removed the morning grogginess his morning coffee seemed to have missed. The storm had blown all through the night and was still battering the coast with wind and rain.

Peter had to check the line on his boat and make sure the bilge pump was kicking on as it was supposed to. The little two horse power motor on the dinghy was having a hard time beating against the wind and waves which kept pushing it back towards the shore. Normally, Peter would reach his boat in under five minutes but this trip had already taken fifteen and he still hadn't quite gotten there yet. Approaching from the leeward side, he was able to slip a line around the rear cleat and secure the dinghy.

The bilge pump appeared to be working properly though there was still a lot of water in the boat from the last deluge. It probably just hadn't made its way into the bilge yet. Peter started the engines and was pleased by their quick response to the turn of the key. He would warm them up to let the battery get a charge but there was no way he was going out today. He went into the cabin then out the front hatch to check the line that held the boat to its mooring. Everything seemed fine but he decided to put out an anchor just for a little insurance. With the anchor set and the line secure, Peter went back into the cabin to check the galley for coffee.

Peter Winthorpe sat at the little table in the galley holding the hot cup of coffee between his hands, enjoying its warmth as well as its aroma. Looking out the window he could see the other boats that were moored in the harbor. They were mostly working boats. There weren't any leaves on the trees that surrounded the harbor on three sides. It was still early spring, long before the season would begin. By summertime the harbor would look like a parking lot. The season meant money. Without the season their little bed and breakfast couldn't survive and he never would have had enough money for this old boat.

His night with Esmerelda tired him out more then usual he thought as he sipped the hot coffee. He was starting to feel his age and wasn't too happy about it. He wasn't sure why he hadn't told her about his vision in the window last night. Maybe it was because he wasn't really sure what the hell he saw. It made him angry just to think about it and he wasn't even sure why. He knew it was an omen of some kind and he didn't like it.

Peter sat in the relative comfort of the cabin as the wind continued to howl contemplating all the thoughts his wandering mind would allow as he finished taking in the warm liquid.

On the return trip the wind was at his back so he wasn't facing the bitter cold spray that bounced off the stern, but halfway back to the shore the deluge came down again. Peter could barely see beyond the front of the dinghy which was a mere five feet away. Inching along, he made it to the beach without a problem.

Peter pulled the dinghy up across the sand past the high water mark, then tied it to a tree just to be safe. Before heading back to the house, he turned to check the boat only to be shocked by the sight of a man standing in his boat. A man with the face he had seen in the window. Peter rubbed the rain from his eyes and when he looked again, he saw no one.

———————————

Esmerelda was busy in the kitchen preparing a nice breakfast for Peter upon his return. French toast with bananas and raisins, cheese omelet, bacon, fresh orange juice and cinnamon buns. She knew he would be extra hungry after the energy he expended last night.

The guests from yesterday had checked out early after a quick coffee and Danish. The house was empty again and would probably stay that way for the next few weeks at least. Then they would be busy. Esmerelda hoped it would be a better summer then the previous season, too many rainy weekends and so cold it never really felt like summer at all.

She heard Peter out in the foyer removing his wet and heavy foul weather gear. She was setting the table when he entered the kitchen. Peter looked pale and fragile, Esmerelda hadn't realized until that moment how much he had aged since they first met.

"Everyting be okay?"

"Yeah, it's just this damn weather, that's all. Smell's good, what'd ya make?" His voice was tired and his eyes had lost their sparkle or something. Esmerelda knew something wasn't right but he wasn't ready to talk about it yet.

"Is da boat okay?" She probed while serving his breakfast. "Dere be mo' juice if you want tit."

"Nah, this is fine." Peter started to pick at the food on his plate but his mind was elsewhere.

"Planet Earth to Petar, Planet Earth to Petar. Come in Petar." She smiled at him as he looked up then continued to eat his meal.

"Sorry, it's just this damn weather. I'm wasting time."

"Don't worry about a ting. Dat treasure ain't going nowhere. It be wherever it be fo mo' den a hundred years. Where it gonna go now?"

"I don't know. I just have a feelin' time's runnin' out."

11

Heading North

Our departure from Key West went without a hitch, almost. The police came by to ask a few questions as we were preparing to leave, but they really didn't seem to be too interested in the answers. I think they just wanted to see the guys that tackled the football team. Since no one was pressing any charges, the team had left the island, we were free to go, even though we were never accused of anything.

Tyler and Jack spent the day getting supplies and stowing them below deck while I checked the lines and sails. I must admit I was more surprised then anyone that we were actually ready to sail on time. Luckily for me, both Jack and Tyler were experienced sailors having grown up with ties to most of the east coast yacht clubs.

We were ready to cast off when we saw Lorraine running towards us along the dock.

"Wait up, you guys!" She was still running but we weren't going anywhere. I stepped off the boat to the dock and she ran right into my arms.

"I just wanted to say goodbye, again and good luck. I'm gonna miss you." She said with a blushing smile.

"Hey, whadda about us?" Jack moaned from back in the cockpit.

"Yeah, I'll miss all of yas. Y'all comin' down next year, right?"

"We'll be back." I said as I watched the afternoon sun brighten her eyes. It felt good to be holding her again.

"Specially you." She said with her eyes locked to mine as she placed a warm, passionate kiss on my lips. Jack started in with the schoolboy hoots but Tyler just sat back and smiled.

We untied the lines and pushed "The Nightwind" out into the marina, then raised her sails and were off. Lorraine stood at the dock waving, she was saying something but we couldn't hear her, we all waved back but no one said a word.

Our first landfall would be around Big Pine Key, though we wouldn't actually leave the boat. It would be dark by then but we should make it. The wind was steady and the seas calm, the storm that was battering the northeast would be long gone by the time we got there.

––––––––––––

It was a long cold spring in the northeast. The kind that made it seem like winter would last forever. The heat wave "The Nightwind" was riding north would finally sweep through the New England area warming the air with the first real taste of summer.

We sailed by our feelings and the wind. Sometimes we sailed through the night only to stay at a port for the next few days. We spent three days in Charleston, South Carolina. The morning we planned to set sail a storm came through, so we spent two more days.

We traveled mostly on the Intercoastal Waterway. That kept us out of the shipping lanes. The water was calmer and the wind pretty steady, though sometimes the wind was blocked and maneuverability for sailing was limited.

The trip went without incident till one night in a bar in Nags Head. Jack was talking with a woman at the bar when a guy came up behind him. After tapping Jack on the shoulder to get his attention, the guy clocks Jack right on the jaw. Jack didn't take his introduction too kindly. When the guy threw his second punch, Jack caught the guy's fist in that massive hand of his and began to crush it till the guy fell to his knees. Then another guy, a friend of the guy Jack was holding, lunged forward but I stepped in his way before he got his momentum up. After that he called me a few choice names then went to take a swing at me but Tyler grabbed his arm on the back swing and sent him reeling into a table. Jack was about to restructure the guy's face he was holding when I grabbed his forearm preventing his punch.

"Forget it, Jack. He ain't worth it."

Friends and strangers at the bar were ready to start a major brawl by now, maybe they did, I don't know we left. A couple of yahoos followed us outside but they stayed by the door. They didn't start to yell obscenities till we were almost out of sight.

The next incident happened while we were crossing the Chesapeake Bay and was far more threatening. We had anchored inside Cape Henry the night before so we could cross in daylight since we would be crossing the shipping lanes.

The morning brought a gray dreary overcast dawn. The wind was calm, less then five knots. It was enough to keep us moving and was bound to pick up as the day progressed. The crossing started at a slow pace. Everything seemed to be going well though our speed was less then desired. Off on the eastern horizon we spotted an oil tanker that was approaching the bay. It seemed the further north we sailed, the further north the track of the tanker took. The tanker was traveling at a steady speed of about fifteen knots. We were doing about eight at the time. It was definitely gaining on us.

After a close watch with all eyes glued on the horizon, we came to the agreement we had passed the line of its present course. We should be safe, but then when it was close enough to smell the aroma of coffee from their bridge, the monstrous ship altered its course to adjust its position to enter the channel. We hastily trimmed the sails to squeak out as much speed as we could with the ship bearing down on us. Luck was with us that day as we surfed away from it on its bow wake just as the sun broke through the clouds, but it was so close Jack threw his bottle of beer against the tanker's hull.

"Remind me to call my attorney at our next port!" Tyler was visibly shaken, we all were, but Tyler was mad as hell.

"What yer gonna do, have a will drawn up?" Jack kidded him as he opened another beer.

"Nah, he'll probably just sue the owner." I added.

"Sue the owner?! Hell, I am the owner. I was almost run down by one of my own god damn boats!"

Jack and I couldn't help but laugh at the irony of the situation, which probably agitated Tyler even more, but he eventually cooled down. Then we all laughed and it felt good. It was good to just be alive.

Tyler made that call to his lawyer too. He had a fax sent to all the ships in his small fleet: to be more conscious of recreational boaters, their paycheck could be onboard.

The remainder of the trip was uneventful. We crossed over the Hudson Canyon with no problems and decided to stay on the ocean till we reached the Shinnecock Inlet. Waiting for the canal locks to open, we fished Shinnecock Bay for flounders and caught enough for dinner.

We sailed into Sag Harbor for supplies about an hour or so before sunset. The sky was already showing signs of a storm coming. Dark clouds were moving towards the southeast from the sound rather quickly and thunder could be heard in the distance. Jack stayed with the boat while Tyler and I went in for our immediate needs. I was hoping to be anchored in Coecles Harbor before the storm hit. No such luck.

The rain started almost as soon as we left the wharf. There was no point in turning back since there was really no place for us to go. Most of the sail would be in protected waters. Only a small portion would be on the relatively open waters of Gardiner's Bay before the harbor channel's entrance.

Once we passed the old Cedar Point Lighthouse things got nasty. Jack hung to the windward side for extra ballast, as Tyler finished reefing the main sail then trimmed the storm jib. I maintained the tiller against the wind and current.

"Look!" We heard Jack's yell overpowering the sound of gusting wind, rain and water smacking the hull. He was pointing towards Gardiner's Island.

We all saw it. There off the northern point of the island, a large barkentine was beating against the wind. Suddenly, the ship jolted and swung around. Its port side was now facing us. The upper part of the main sail snapped and went crashing to the deck bringing down more sails and rigging with it. The ship rapidly began listing heavily to its starboard side, then it faded from sight as if it was never there.

We held our stares and didn't say anything. A large wave washing over our bow brought us all back to the peril of our immediate predicament. In a few minutes we sailed into the entrance of the harbor in complete silence. By the time we had the sails down and anchored, the storm had passed.

12

Big Plans

Macy sat in his cabin brooding over his future. Bennington played the game well, Macy had to respect him for that. Most men would have crumbled but Bennington came back stronger. Macy felt he was stronger now too. He had found a new power in his black magic that had given him the strength to carry on. The time in the Mexican prison had eaten away at him. He would rather have been killed then confined in that stinking cell. Their escape proved that point. It was a one in a million shot they would make it out of the country alive, but they did and became rich men again.

Macy decided this job was going to be his last. He'd take his money and go to Bangkok where he could live like a king. All his fantasies would be realities and realities pure pleasure. Macy was in his dream when the knock came on the door. He opened it and was more than surprised to see Bennington standing there.

"We need to talk Macy." Bennington said walking right in.

"Sure, Doc. Anything you want." Macy rubbed the three day growth of a beard on his chin. Bennington offered him the bottle he was still carrying. Macy took a swig and handed it back.

"Have you given any thought as to how we're gonna get into the country?" Doc took another swig of rum himself.

"Not yet. There's plenty of time still." Macy was wondering what Doc was up to. Planning was Macy's area of the partnership, Bennington was supposed to handle business matters.

"Well, I have. We're gonna need another boat, a fast one. Something that can out run the Coast Guard and blend in with the tourists. Something with New York registration numbers on it."

"Makes sense. The numbers are no problem." Macy paused, rubbed his chin again as if in thought. "You've been giving this a lot of thought, why?"

"Can you arrange it?"

"Yeah, sure. What's the hurry?"

"I want the boat as soon as possible, before we get closer to our destination."

Macy was getting aggravated. He didn't like not being answered but he thought Doc's plan made sense. He thought he knew a likely place to get a boat in the next day or so.

Bennington seemed pleased by Macy's responses, leaving him to make the arrangements.

On his way back to his cabin, Bennington ran into Sheraton Quinn, on his way to report their position. Sheraton still didn't have an exact fix yet but figured it would be to his benefit to keep Bennington informed of the approximate distance traveled. He speculated they would be near Bermuda in a day or so. Bennington thanked him for the information and waited till he was gone before changing his direction for the lower decks of the ship.

Before him now was a door he had only seen once before in his life. He listened for any sounds being made on the other side, then swung it open quickly causing it to slam against the wall.

"Hello Amanda. How are you today?"

13

Ghost Ships

From down below, I could hear Jack and Tyler talking about what we had witnessed during the storm. Tyler was cooking the fish on my small hibachi while I boiled some corn on the cob and potatoes. Jack was tending the wine bucket making sure the wine was cold and everyone's glass was full.

"So what do you think it was then?" Jack inquired while refilling Tyler's glass.

"I'm really not sure, old boy, but I read once about how certain atmospheric conditions could cause illusions on the water. Kinda like mirages. Things that were really a great distance away would appear quite close, sort of magnified." He took a long drink of wine. "Maybe it was something like that." Tyler was grasping for straws. He flipped the fish as I came up the companionway. I could see from the look on his face Jack wasn't buying it.

"Everything's almost ready. How's the fish?" I showed Jack my empty glass which he promptly refilled.

"Right on schedule, old boy." Raising his glass before taking another sip of wine. "Tell me, what do you think it was?"

The stars burned brightly in the evening sky as the boat swung gently at anchor. The storm had passed and so had its intensity leaving in its wake a calm with the sensitivity of a raw nerve. I sat back relaxing in the cockpit opposite Jack and Tyler. After taking a long sip of the ice cold wine I saw they were still waiting for my answer. I took another sip and told them.

"I think it was a ghost ship."

As I expected they both burst into laughter. The expressions on their faces were amusing, a mixture of disbelief and confusion.

"Surely you're joking." Tyler said with a chuckle.

"Actually, I'm not." Feeling a little awkward about my response, I took another long sip of wine and shoved the glass towards Jack for a refill. Jack watched my face as he poured the wine.

"Tyler, he ain't jokin'." Jack smiled and put a fresh bottle in the wine bucket.

Tyler eyed me over his glass of wine. He flipped the fish again and said, "These look done."

Jack and I brought up the rest of the entree and dinner was served under the rising moon on the calm waters of Coecles Harbor. The wind had died but the warmth of the early summer's breeze was still in the air. We toasted to summer.

"Let the feast begin!" Nothing fazed Jack, at least not for long. Life just went on, so why not enjoy it.

Tyler's mood was pensive.

"So, you really think it was a ghost ship." His tone was sarcastic and mocking. He seemed agitated, even Jack picked up on it.

"Tyler, relax. Believe me, there are things in this world you wouldn't believe unless they walked up and bit you, and some of them will."

"So, I suppose you thought it was a ghost ship too?"

"You saw it too. What's your opinion?"

"I don't know. A mirage, an illusion brought on by fear or drinking too much."

"Maybe mass hypnosis, perhaps. We all saw it." Now Jack's tone had taken on a sarcastic air. "Besides none of us had anything to drink since we left Cape May, three days ago. So how do you explain that."

"I can't explain any of it!"

Tyler mood was growing worst. He seemed to be avoiding eye contact with me, waiting for a rational explanation he could except. He knew I believed what I had said. Now he was starting to realize Jack believed it too.

"Tyler, all I can say is Jack is right. There are things in this world you'll never believe till it happens to you."

"And it just happened." Jack chimed in.

"That's right." I waited as Jack filled all our glasses. In the distance from another boat at anchor the low haunting tones of a clarinet could be heard drifting across the calm still water.

"I never told ya what happen to me in 'Nam', did I?"

"No, you didn't." Tyler was drinking wine like water but it wasn't having any calming effect on his ediginess. He took a big gulp of wine and sat back with his eyes to the stars, waiting for more of the inevitable.

"Yeah, Tyler. I bet you didn't know the captain here was in the special forces. Assassins, espionage, you know, whatever."

"Really?" Tyler's head snapped forward with burning interest.

"Yeah, really. Tell him."

"How did you get involved with that. You don't seem like the type."

"I'm not, really. I was only with them towards the end, before we pulled out. I got into some trouble in Saigon with a couple of girls that were being forced into prostitution."

"What happened?" Tyler appeared more at ease, I don't know if it was the story or the wine kicking in.

"I had a little talk with their pimp, and well one thing led to another and before I knew it the army was investigating me. They found out I had an extensive background in martial arts. That combined with a marksmanship record in my shooting scores convinced them to turn me into a killing machine. I went along with it to stay out the clink."

"What happened to the girls?" Jack busted in.

"Went back to turning tricks. I think there was someone on the inside who…"

"So, what's that got to do with ghost ships?" Tyler requested as he refilled his own glass.

"Nothing, really. Just splaining how I got there. What I wanted to tell you about was a mission inside Loas." Holding up my glass for a refill.

"We had been sent in for an exchange of prisoners. There's no record of the exchange. Intelligence had gotten all they wanted from the package to be traded. Our job was to retrieve our parcel then terminate the exchange commission. Only we didn't know the drug lord they worked for made other arrangements with a certain CIA spook who organized the exchange. We walked into an ambush. The captain thought he had planned for every possibility but the man we came for was already dead.

"We were deeper behind enemy lines then any previous mission had attempted before. We all scrambled for whatever cover we could find. We were pinned in a crossfire. I couldn't tell if any of our squad had been hit, but I could see our package on his belly snaking his way towards his own people. I had him in my sights and was about to squeeze the trigger when the top of his head flew back in a violent snap showering the landscape in brain matter. His own people shot him, they didn't want him either."

In the dead calm of the night even the sound of water lapping the hull was absent.

"I looked around as the bullets were flying all around us and saw the captain in the distance signaling to us the way out. The squad inched its way back to our lines. Whenever we thought the situation was hopeless the captain showed us the way. It was the only time we saw him, always in the distance leading the way."

"We made it back with three casualties, almost half the team. We didn't find out till then the captain had been the first to die, caught in the ambush. We never would have made it back without him. We all saw him. None of us every told the brass that part of the assignment or that we swore to each other. No matter what the circumstances, if we ever ran across that bastard from the CIA, we'd rip his heart out and dance on it till rigor mortis took hold of his useless body."

We sat in a moon lit silence listening to the portentous sound of the woodwind capture the air in its eerie grip. Jack stared at the stars perhaps thinking of his own ghosts in the closet. Tyler sipped at his wine as I watched a lone cloud momentarily block the moon's glowing light.

"Did any of you ever find him?" Tyler questioned in a somber voice.

"No. And there's only two of us left."

"What do you mean, old boy?"

"Two of them are dead. Neither one of natural causes. Sean Nolan, they found his burnt body in a car wreck outside of San Paulo. He was down there on business. The coroner couldn't imagine how the crash could have twisted his neck that way. Carlos renounced his citizenship and went back to Mexico. Had a great little business going. Sanchez Express, a whole fleet of buses that ran tourists to the ruins. On his way to his first million in the bank he decides to hang himself."

Jack was back to filling our glasses with the last of the wine.

"So why are you so sure this was a ghost ship?"

"Probably because there've been sightings like this for the last two hundred years or so."

"Really?" Tyler's curiosity had peaked. When that happened his thirst for answers was hard to satisfy.

"Well, there's one story about a bunch of fishermen who saw two ships doing battle but never heard the cannons fire even though they were close enough to see men on deck and smoke from the guns. Then there's the story about a fishing boat about to be rammed broadside but the ship disappeared when it should have made impact."

"Yeah. Remember that island over there, they say Captain Kidd buried treasure on it." Jack was swept with excitement as tried to pour more wine from the empty bottle still in his hand.

"This whole area has a history of pirates, rum runners, treasures, ghosts, witches, whatever you want."

"You know, I got drunk once with a guy down in South America who was talking about a treasure he was looking for. He didn't know where it was but he said one day he was gonna find it. I don't think he was talking about Kidd's treasure though, I don't know." Jack was starting to ramble. We were all pretty tired and decided to call it a night. The melody of the clarinet was drifting away now as the night wind started to stir the air.

14

Destiny

Amanda Paige sobbed heavily with her face buried into the shoulder of "Doc" Bennington. He had covered her with his jacket, though she was neither cold nor embarrassed, and had his arm around her.

"You're pretty emotional for a zombie." Casper said with more then a touch of sarcasm in his voice.

"You gotta get me outta here. he's crazy. He's gonna kill me." Her sobbing increased again.

"He's not going to kill you. He would have done that already, if that were his plan." Bennington held her closer, offering her the rum he still carried. She declined.

"I can't take you out of here. Not yet, anyway."

"Whadda yer mean?" She was angry and pulled away from him.

"I need you here for now. So you can find out just what it is his plans are."

"His plans are to fuck me like a fuckin' rag doll whenever the fuck he feels like it. That's his fuckin' plan!" She was mad and as she spoke droplets of spittle shot from her mouth.

"Look, you help me and I'll see you get back to America."

"I've heard that before. Besides, how the hell am I suppose to survive in here. The bastard hasn't even fed me since he dumped me in here."

"Zombies aren't supposed to get hungry." Bennington amused himself.

"Well, I ain't no fuckin' zombie!" Amanda definitely didn't see the humor in it.

"Relax dear. I'll see you get food and water. You just see what you can find out. I'll be back." He took his coat from her and walked to the door. Casper turned to face her in the doorway, viewing her as she stood unabashed at the center of the room.

"You're still quite beautiful, my dear. Don't do anything to spoil it."

Then she was alone.

"Thanks a lot. You bastard."

———————

Casper Bennington stood on the deck of the "Enya" observing the evening twilight turn to darkness. It was a magnificent blend of orange and purple that glowed and reflected off the rolling swells of a calm sea.

Doc took another swig from the rum bottle but it was finally empty. He threw it over the side and watched it sink to depths unknown. He thought back to when he was a kid stuffing notes into bottles. He wondered if they ever washed up anywhere and if anyone ever read them. The days when he used to play pirate.

The aroma of marijuana drifted on the air interrupting Bennington's reminiscences of his youth. Sheraton Quinn was nearby and Bennington was looking for him. Doc didn't even know his name.

"Hey you! I want to talk to you." Bennington made his way over to where he saw the billows of smoke coming from.

"My name be, Quinn, Sheraton Quinn, Mistar Bennington." Sheraton was only slightly annoyed. He was used to the way

Bennington and Macy treated the crew as being less than human. He took a long drag on his joint not taking his eyes off the sunset.

"Well, Mr. Quinn, I have a job for you." Bennington explained to Sheraton how he wanted him to sneak food to Amanda.

"You be crazy, mon. Mistar Macy would kill me fo dat."

"There'll be more money in it for you."

"What I gonna do wif money if I be dead, tell me dat." Sheraton inhaled the last of the joint then flicked the roach into the sea as Bennington upped the ante.

"What would you say to a piece of the action?"

"Dis woman, why's she so important?" Sheraton looked out to sea as night over took the sky with stars.

"That's my concern. We got a deal or not?"

"Okay mon, I keep da little girl fed." Bennington shook his hand but Sheraton didn't feel anymore secure about it.

Bennington said he would try to keep Macy occupied while the food was brought. He wanted her fed now. Sheraton headed to the galley to see what he could rustle up while Bennington headed towards Macy's cabin. Doc listened at the door to make sure Macy was there, then waited a few minutes before bursting in unannounced.

"Well, if it ain't Doc Bennington stopping in to see me again. I hear you're quite the social butterfly these days. Been all over the ship, haven't you? So, what do I owe this pleasant surprise to?" Macy leaned against the wall that backed his bunk. Bennington noticed he was reading a book on the occult. He had a sinking feeling that Macy had seen his visit to Amanda but he let it pass. What else could he do?

"Cut the crap, Macy. Did you make any arrangements yet?"

"Not yet, but I've been thinking about it. I figured I could slip into Bermuda with a couple of boys. I'm sure we can find what we're looking for there. Something so fast the wind will rip your hair out." Bennington wasn't amused by Macy's little joke since he had gone bald years ago.

"Alright. How long till we get to Bermuda?"

"A couple of days. That will give us time to repaint the boat and give it new numbers before we reach New York."

"Okay, sounds good. You got any rum around here?"

Macy went over to a foot locker, took out a bottle of Bounties he had picked up in St. Lucia and handed it to Bennington. Macy explained how he planned to slip in and out of Bermuda which seemed to please Bennington that things were being thought out for a change. They traded the bottle back and forth. It almost seemed like the old days when they trusted each other with their lives. Maybe they were corrupted by the greed or maybe it just happened to people, no matter what the circumstances.

Bennington stayed for forty five minutes and half a bottle. He had forgotten the original reason he had come. Before he left he told Macy directly,

"I don't want any problems on this one. We'd never get out of an American jail."

"Amen to that."

———————

Sheraton Quinn watched as Amanda Paige stuffed more fried chicken down her throat then he had ever seen one skinny little white girl eat. In fact, he didn't know many men that could put away that much food. She washed it down by alternating between a bottle of water and a bottle of red wine.

Sheraton lit up another cigar size joint as he eyeballed the naked blonde beauty eat. He was hoping she was almost done so he could get out before anyone knew he had been there.

"You gonna smoke dat ting all by yourself?"

Sheraton offered her the joint which she took a long drag on. Blowing out a large cloud of smoke, she took another drag then passed it back.

"Where we headed?" she questioned trying to hold the smoke in her lungs.

"Dey say 'women on a ship be bad luck'. Since you be here, noting be normal no mo. What deez men want you fo?" He passed the joint back to Amanda.

"I don't know! Just a good fuck, I guess."

"Nobody be dat good to cause all dis trouble. So, till I know fo sure. I won't be answering no questions. I bring mo food in da morning." He stuck the remainder of the joint between his lips while he removed all signs of food and water from the room.

"I be back when I can. Don't worry, pretty lady, everting gonna be okay."

Amanda Paige was alone again. She sat down in the corner next to the engine room. The drone from the diesels in the warm little room put her to sleep in minutes.

15

❦

Market Place

At the market place Esmerelda scrutinized the produce with a careful eye. As a child she had been taught fresh vegetables were an important part of the life force. They made you strong. To eat less than the best would deprive the soul. So, with meticulous determination Esmerelda chose what she wanted and tossed back the rest.

Esmerelda went to the market everyday since she was seven years old. When she was a child on her native island it was the most exciting place in the world to her. She would wander from stall to stall gazing at the various items for sale, hoping one day to have a stall of her own. Then she met Peter Winthorpe. She was all of nineteen at the time and Peter was as dashing a figure as she had ever seen. He had been around the world several times, to places Esmerelda only saw in her dreams. He offered her adventure like she had never dared to imagine…and travel, but she was afraid to put too much credence in his words, afraid to trust this stranger who could be gone tomorrow.

Under the light of a full moon they drank the better part of a bottle of rum in between passionate bouts of love making. When the bottle was done so was Peter and he lay passed out on the beach. Esmerelda lay with him watching the stars that dusted the sky with its limitless points of light. The moon hung close to the horizon when Peter started to stir. He startled Esmerelda, acting like a man possessed he began to spit out words only half of which she could make out. Gold was one of them.

Reaching for her bag amongst their pile of clothes, Esmerelda pulled out a small bottle she had nicknamed "Love Potion Number Nine." Half aphrodisiac, half truth serum, she put the bottle to Peter's lips as he involuntarily drank some of the liquid. She rubbed the mixture onto his lips and nostrils while he inhaled. When he awoke her mouth was on him as he became erect, the pleasure cleared his mind to concentrate. As the frenzied ecstasy bordered on exultation she mounted him and while her slow rhythmic movement again built the sensation to the point of uncontrolled containment, she questioned his unprotected soul. He told her everything, and when she had finished with him he told her more. When he was done he knew he couldn't live without her. She was part of him now and she wanted to be there. She showed him the way in ways he never believed possible but they found what they were searching for each time. They had been together ever since and she never used that black magic potion on him again.

Now her mind returned to the thoughts that most occupied her mind of recent days.

Her worry was of Peter, he had always been obsessed by his hunt for the treasure but lately it became a mania out of control. He was agitated and nervous. She found him talking to himself in his preoccupied state. He was pushing himself to the limit without a direction to go in. Esmerelda knew this was not in character for the man she knew so well. One who had stood strong against so many odds all his life.

From the time Peter Winthorpe first came into possession of the patriarchal log books he followed the signs. A trip that spanned thousands of miles. It was never easy. Time had been his biggest enemy, then he met Esmerelda.

Then the enemies he made in Brazil found him again, only now he traveled with a woman. A woman with a power that helped save them. Men died in the Yucatan, on all sides of the fence, but Peter and Esmerelda escaped. Now all his enemies were catching up to him again, even new ones yet unknown.

"I must do someting," Esmerelda whispered aloud. "I must do someting berry bad."

With her mind in its own state of preoccupation she left the market with the goods she purchased. As she walked back to the bed and breakfast, past the Inn The Middle Pub, Jack Rogin and Tyler Martin were having drinks with a bit of lunch totally unaware of the evil lurking in the deep corners of the Voodoo priestess's mind right outside the door.

16

⚜

Last Call

The air held the warmth of spring with its grip except down close to the water where the slightest breeze grabbed all the liquid's chill. My back felt it. It was a beautiful day with only a few passing clouds casting their shadows as they crept along. With the "Nightwind" secured in Sag Harbor, I was rowing in to pick up supplies.

Jack and Tyler had decided to stay aboard till the weekend had passed, then they would find other accommodations. Tyler expressed interest in spending the entire summer. He had nowhere to be and most of his business concerns could be taken care of over the phone.

"Thank god for e-mails and faxes!" Tyler elated. "They save me hours of useless travel time, for papers I just hand over to my lawyers anyway. Once or twice a year I may drop in on an office just to shake them up." He paused and contemplated what he said. "What are your plans, Jack?"

"I really hadn't thought about it. This part of Long Island ain't exactly where I'd like to be. It's just too damn close to home." Jack lapsed a second before saying, "There's a lot of people I won't want to run into."

"You grew up in the Hampton's, didn't you?" I was pretty sure that was the story I heard. I was trying to make another point though.

"Yeah, I grew up here. In a big old place on Gin Lane," he raised his little pinky as he toasted with the bottle of beer he was using to wash down his morning eggs, "So what?"

"So, I'm just asking."

"The family tossed me when I was eighteen, well not really. First they sent me to college. Then they tossed me out. My father said it was because I was a drunk, but he was just pissed. He couldn't sit around with his buddies at the country club bragging how his son played pro ball. Anyway, there's too many Rogins out here or friends of there of." He straddled the next hurdle. "I don't want to see them and I'm sure they don't want to see me."

"I understand your problem, Jack. But what are the chances you'll run into any of them on Shelter Island?"

Jack raised his eyebrow at me. I didn't get a reply till after I saw Tyler's slightest grin.

"Good point. I'll keep that in mind." Jack answered as he pondered the thought.

"You know, Jack, I was thinking about that ship we saw last night, and I was wondering if there was any way we could find out more about it." Tyler had the look in his eye of a man who was pondering the thought of an adventure. Jack was quick to respond, always searching for extracurricular activities himself. They both eyed me.

"Look guys, I'd love to join your little expedition but actually I'm here on business."

"You're kiddin'." Jack sarcastically bellowed.

"No, really. I made a deal before I left for Key West, to run day cruises for one of the inns. If fact, that one up on the hill." I answered with a wave of the hand that no one seemed to respond in any way to. "I made a deal with the manger. I have to meet him to work out the details. We had a verbal agreement, and I, for one, plan to honor it."

They both sat in silence till Tyler offered a toast to my good fortune in my business endeavor. Jack reluctantly chorused in.

After Jack and Tyler departed to explore the island by foot, I set sail for Sag Harbor. Sailing the boat alone after so long gave the boat a larger than normal feel. I was going to miss having those guys around all the time. In some ways I felt I was deserting them but I knew that was ridiculous. The money I would make for the summer would probably amount to less than either one of them had in their pockets right now, but it could hold me over for the winter. It was just the luck of the draw, as rich as they were from birth, I was as equally poor. I didn't have any complaints though, that's just the way it was.

The season wasn't officially in gear for another week and the streets of Sag Harbor were still rather empty. Winter had lasted long into spring in the northeast which hadn't exactly given the tourist trade a jump start. Everyone was hoping for a great summer, especially after last year's disaster. It rained at least one day of every weekend, if not two, except for two weekends when it was cold. Business was off between forty and fifty percent for the entire east end. A dry hot summer could hurt the farmers but it could save hundreds of small businesses involved in the tourist trade.

After getting the supplies, I stopped in at Schooner's to see if Bill was still working the bar. Bill wasn't around, he had taken a week off before he started his summer hours, which would be unpredictable to say the least. I was talking to Mark who up till now I only knew as the other bartender and he was making me feel old.

Mark was only a year or so older then me but what little was left of his gray hair made him look a good ten years older.

"Does Dan come around anymore?"

"No way! Bill kicked him out on New Year's Eve after he started a fight and busted up the place. The cops came and everything."

"Figures. Do you know where I might find him?"

"No idea. Haven't seen him since. Why he owe you money or something?"

"Yeah, something. Not that I ever really expected I see it again, but it was worth a try."

"Too bad." Mark started stacking the glasses he had been drying back into their positions on the shelf. When he was done he emptied the rest of the margarita left in the shaker into my glass.

"Whatta 'bout Jimmy? He been 'round lately?" I questioned before sipping my drink.

"You didn't heard about Jimmy? That made the news! CNN!" "No shit! What'd he do now?" Just the thought of some of the stunts this guy had pulled brought a smile to my face. I can't imagine how my face must have changed as the words Mark spoke registered deep in my being:

"He committed suicide. I'm surprised you didn't know. He took the cops on a high speed chase first and lost them. When they found him, he was dead. Overdosed. He left a note saying 'Life caught up to me but the cops couldn't.'"

I left Schooner's dazed. The spirit had been ripped from my soul. After thanking Mark for the drink, he wouldn't take my money. I told him to let Bill know I was in town and would be back to see them. From there I got my supplies and a case of tequila with the money I had left from Key West. So with only small change left in my pocket, I was rowing my booty back to the "Nightwind".

The sun had sunk low but it was still daylight. The shadow of the trees that lined the shore along Coecles Harbor cast their dark cloud across the water covering the boat. I had finished about three quarters of a bottle of tequila when I realized it would have been more appropriate if it had been Southern Comfort, Jim's favorite, but it was the thought that counted. Lying low in the cockpit hearing voices calling I took another shot and sucked down a lime.

"Damn!" The thought wouldn't leave my mind. "Jimmy was the last one. I never thought he would end it like that. Hell, he was the guy who said, 'live it or live with it.' When the hell did things go wrong?"

Suddenly from over the side I heard, "Hey, what the hell's going on out here. We've been yellin' for half an hour."

I couldn't help but laugh when I stuck my head over the gunwale at the sight of Jack swimming in his underwear.

"Well, you gonna help me up or not? This water's freezing." Once Jack was in the boat, though it took awhile cause I couldn't stop laughing, I rowed the dinghy to shore to pick up Tyler. The exercise straightened me out a little. Once back on board the "Nightwind" I was feeling much better. Jack had put on some warm clothes but still had a blanket wrapped around him, making him look like some sort of medieval sorcerer.

"Did Tyler tell ya the news?"

"I thought I'd wait till we were all together." Tyler admitted while Jack handed out beers from the cooler which I declined. He put the beer back and picked up the almost empty bottle of tequila.

"Private party?" He asked sarcastically.

"I'll tell yer about it later." I caught the glance they gave each other and was thankful they didn't push it.

"So, what's the big news flash?"

"Tell'em, Tyler. You're so much more better with words."

"Quite." Tyler eyed Jack dubiously. "Well, old boy, Jack and I did a little investigating on that ship we saw last night. Seems you two were right when you said the area had a history of pirates, ghosts and other phenomenon."

"You're tellin' me you guys spent the day at the library?"

"Yeah, but we did sneak in our own refreshments." Jack held up a flask that was close to a foot long.

"We started out at a place called Inn The Middle, but the way Casey says hello, the locals didn't take us serious though. Casey suggested we try the library, so we did. They had a lot of interesting articles on local history, including the sightings you mentioned and a few others. There wasn't much on what we were looking for though. Other than it was believed to be a whaler named "Corona" whose home port was Sag Harbor. She was on her way out to sea after having just been refitted and scraped. They think she decided to return to port when a sudden storm came up the coast. Must have been a hurricane from the sounds of the damage it did around the area. There's suppose to be a book with more details but it's constantly on loan to someone. We were the first people to ask for it since he had checked it out. He's had it for the last three years."

"We were thinking about renting some diving equipment and checking it out. Wanna join us?"

"I can't." My head was still groggy but I seemed to remember something about that area on my charts. I went to get one, chart #67, Gardiners Bay.

"Oh, I forgot. You're gonna be working." Jack's voice sounded honestly dejected at the thought of my absence.

"It's not that. I have a bad ear I can't dive, but if I'm not mistaken you can't dive there either."

"Why not?"

"I'll show you." I spread out the chart on the cabin top and lit a couple of lanterns. The twilight had passed into darkness without our noticing. "I thought so. See, here's Gardiners Island, up here off the point is right about where we saw the ship. The area's known as the "Ruins". The army used it for gunnery practice during the wars. It's still a restricted area. There's probably undetonated shells down there or somethin'. Besides, anything that was down there has been blown to smithereens."

"There goes that plan!" Jack popped another cold one.

"I won't totally discount it yet. There might be a way around the problem." Tyler emptied his bottle than looked around. "Anybody hungry besides me? Why don't we go over to that inn over there. I hear the food is very good."

"Tyler, I'm broke."

"No problem. My treat for all the good times."

We arrived late but Tyler tipped the cook and staff into staying though they did inform us of a slightly limited menu. We placed our orders with a waitress whose very young pretty face was accented by her short blonde hair that was pulled into a bun. When she came back with two ice buckets for the wine she told us our appetizers would be out in a moment. We thanked her then toasted to a great summer. The lull in the activity gave me the opportunity to temporarily excuse myself.

Crossing the dining room floor my exit brought me to the lobby and the front desk.

"Is Brian around?" Brian was the manager I had the agreement with and was suppose to meet with upon my return.

"I'm sorry, Brian left a few months ago. Moved back to San Francisco after the new owner brought the place." The girl at the desk smiled, I knew the face but for the life of me I couldn't remember her name.

"Who's the new owner?"

"Parker Webster. If you want to leave a message I'll see that he gets it."

"Nay, I'll come back. When is he usually around?"

"Usually from about ten till four…but he could pop in any time." I thanked her for her time and headed for the bar then remembered I didn't have any money. Another bartender named Bill greeted me. He said he didn't recollect my name but the face was familiar.

"Oh yeah, I remember you now." Bill looked like a college kid that had missed graduation. The crow's feet accentuated the tired look in his eyes.

"What'll you have?"

"Sorry, nothin'. I just remembered I'm busted."

"Don't worry. It's on the house." I told him a margarita. While he filled a glass he continued the conversation. "You were supposed to be working here this summer, weren't you?"

"Yeah, I was. I hear there's new management." I observed the frown on Bill's face as he began talking.

"You heard that right."

"I take it you're not too happy with him."

"No one is. The first thing he did was lay off twenty percent of the staff. Totally at random. It's not just that we're pissed, it's hurting business. The regular clientele that come here aren't getting the…satisfaction they're used to. We just don't have the people." He poured the remaining shaker into my glass. "You were supposed to take them sailing. Right?"

"Yeah."

"Would have been a great idea. Good for business, but this guy just sees it as an expense. He's gonna run this place into the ground."

Finishing my drink, I thanked Bill and told him we would probably stop in after dinner. He told me to hurry, if there was less then four people at the bar he had to close early. When I left he was alone again.

———————————

After dinner we headed back to the boat. The bar had closed early but Bill lent us some triple sec and a bottle of lime juice. At first he was going to join us then remembered he was working the early shift in the morning. He had no problem accepting our rain check for another time.

While Tyler and I sat back watching the clouds drift across the sky, Jack went below to mix up some margaritas. In one hand I held the nearly empty bottle of tequila that was still in the cockpit. I could feel Tyler watching me even as the darkness of a blocked out moon crept over us.

"What seems to be the trouble, old boy?" Tyler asked as Jack handed out the first round of drinks. Jack remained silent as we all raised our glasses.

"Gentlemen, today I found out a good friend of mine is dead, I spent my very last dollar and the job I was supposed to have here is history."

The only sound was the water lapping the hull as we sat there in silence.

Watching the lights being extinguished one by one in the houses, we all knew it was late as the shore grew darker.

"Who died?" I heard Jack's voice through the shadowy glow of the moon sounding more somber then I had ever heard it before.

"A guy I knew a long time. Offed himself…so they say." I took a long drink but it didn't wash away anything. "He was the type of guy who you'd never think would do something like that. What's really weird though, that story I told you last night. He was there. Now I'm the last one left." Silently I pondered that thought. "I don't think I ever told that story to anyone before."

"You know you're not respon…"

"Can it, Tyler. I know I'm not responsible. It's just…hell, I don't even know what it is. Maybe sometimes life just makes me feel too old."

The silence in the boat drown out any other noise that wanted to intrude. Jack got up and relit a few of the lanterns before refilling our glasses, none of which were empty.

"So whatta yer gonna do now?"

Subconsciously I might have heard the question but consciously my mind blacked out like darkness filling a room at the last flicker of the candle's flame.

"What was I gonna do?" repeated in my mind over and over.

17

Landfall

At seven miles out the light house on Montauk Point was the first sight of America "Doc" Bennington had seen in a decade. With mixed emotions he watched as its distinctive lines rose on the horizon. Dawn's early light simmered off the starboard side as the 43 foot Scarab thundered across the calm water of the Atlantic. "Doc" could hardly hear Macy's voice above the roar of the triple Merc 600's.

"So…whadda ya think? Fast enough for ya?"

"Doc" took a swig from the bottle that had been at his side since the beginning of this particular 'odyssey', only now it was Jack Daniels. The rum had run out half a world away.

"As long as you think it's fast enough!" "Doc" shouted back.

Macy, who had been cruising at two thirds throttle, pushed the lever to the max. The boat lifted as the engines torn through the water. Macy laughed as Bennington's fingers dug into the seat.

"Okay! You proved your point!" "Doc" took another swig of sour mash as Macy eased off the throttle.

"This boat can out run anything that might come after us."

"What if they got the same boat?" "Doc" was still worried about entering "the States" again.

"You don't hafta worry about that. The Coast Guard ain't gonna get the bucks for one of these!"

"But, what about all the attention this boat is gonna attract?"

"What?!"

"I said, 'what about all the attention this boat is gonna attract?"

"That's what I'm figuring. We'll be so obvious people will be straining not to notice us. Remember, this the playground of the rich and famous. We'll just be another face in the crowd."

They were traveling so fast they were already rounding Montauk Point into Block Island Sound. In a few more minutes they would pass Gardiners Island then Shelter Island into Northwest Harbor on their way to Sag Harbor. Both men sat in silence as they cruised closer to their destination. Thinking about all the money they could make didn't make it any easier. It was a precarious position for both men. Each had his own skeletons in the closet.

Each wondered what the other man's were, and how they could best use them to their advantage. In the end survival was all that really mattered.

Macy paid an assistant harbor master a couple of thousand dollars for an unregistered slip to keep the boat in for a couple of days. With the bills already in his hand the kid didn't ask any questions. He would have done it for a lot less. He'd take care of everything. Money still talked in America. The language was a little more eloquent but the response was the same. A few days was all it would take they hoped, if not they were ready for the long run too.

Bennington watched as Macy secured the boat finishing the last drop of Old No. 7. He knew he would need more liquid courage as he tossed the open bottle into the water watching the air bubbles break the surface as it sank.

"I'm going into town. We need to find a man named Lamar Lorre. Look around and see what you can dig up." Then as an after thought "Doc" added. "And remember, this ain't no banana republic. And I don't want him hurt. I'll see you in a couple of hours."

Macy watched as "Doc" walked away. Smiling Macy figured he didn't need Bennington anymore. He'd just find Lamar, but when he looked up again Bennington was standing over him.

"I've changed my mind. We better stick together. Just in case." Now it was Bennington who was smiling. An evil grin that Macy knew exactly what it meant.

"Okay, I'll be right with yer." It didn't matter that much to Macy. When the time came it would all work out the same.

Fifteen minutes later they blended into the rest of the east end tourists, drifting from bar to bar looking for Lamar or anyone who knew him. Those that did weren't too happy to admit it. It seemed he owed everyone money. Lamar was generally known as a back stabbing little weasel. After paying a couple of his tabs hoping to get information they weren't any closer to finding his whereabouts.

"We traveled half around the globe for this shit!" Macy was getting angrier with every dead end they came up against. "Even if we do find this clown, what makes him so important?"

"He knows where Winthorpe is." "Doc's" voice was calm as he watched for Macy's reaction.

"The bastard's here! With that black whore of his?!"

"Yep. That's why we're here."

"Why the hell didn't you tell me?"

"I didn't want to spoil the surprise." The sarcastic tone in Bennington's voice didn't go unnoticed but Macy had other thoughts on his mind. None of which were legal or civilized.

"But who's this Lamar character? How do we know if we can trust him?"

"We can't. He's my brother."

As the "Enya" drifted lazily twenty miles out to sea the morning sun had risen high above the decks filling them with the golden light of a still early morn. Sheraton Quinn had decided it would be safe to let Amanda on deck for awhile while the boss men were gone. Where was she gonna go? The crew had known of her existence for some time now though this was the first time anyone had seen her.

Amanda's eyes squinted in the glare as she came on deck. Though she never had an ounce of fat on her she had lost weight since her imprisonment. With the oversize clothes Sheraton had given her she appeared frail, but alive and determined to stay that way.

"I can't believe it! We're finally here!" It was the first time Sheraton had seen her smile.

"Dat's right, mon." Sheraton said while inhaling the cigar size joint he was lighting. "Long I land be right over dat horizon."

"So what are we waiting for. Let's go!"

"Can't mon. No way of gettin' dere." He let out a large cloud of smoke which he had been holding in his lungs then took another drag before handing the joint to Amanda.

"Whadda yer mean? We'll take the boat!"

"No way, mon. We take dis boat in doze watars and we be doin' da jail time a long time."

"So what are we supposed to do? Sit here and rot!" Her smile was gone as she handed the smoke back.

"Don't ju be worrin', little lady. Someting gonna happen, cause America be waitin' fo Sheraton Quinn." He smiled his big yellow grin. Amanda couldn't help but smile back.

"I put that little prick's ass in jail two nights ago! It's bad enough I let him sucker me for a two hundred buck tab, but then he starts bustin' up the place. I kicked his ass myself. Nobody pulls that shit in my bar! Nobody!" The bar man was an ex marine who had kept himself in pretty good shape over the years. He didn't like the looks of the two men asking questions about one of the town's particularly notorious lowlifes. He definitely didn't like the snide smile Macy gave him.

"You got a problem with that, mister?"

"No," Macy scratched the back of his neck as he looked around the bar, "but two hundred says you can't kick my ass." Macy's tone was threatening as he stared into the man's eyes.

"Put your money on the bar, friend, and we'll see what yer got."

Macy tossed two hundred dollar bills on the bar which the bartender matched from the cash register. Bennington moved away to a stool at the end of the bar. The place was empty except for two other men who had been talking to the bartender when "Doc" and Macy had come in.

The bartender hopped the bar to impress upon Macy he was messing with the wrong guy. He stood less then a foot in front of Macy and about six inches taller.

Macy smiled his snide little smile again. "What makes you think a pussy like you is gonna stop me from takin' your money too?"

"Fuck you!" With that the ex marine took a swing at Macy and missed entirely. Bennington looked at his watch as the bartender took another swing. He never saw Macy move but felt the back of his head crash to the hardwood floor. He lay there motionless as Macy went to execute a move that could have either crippled him or killed him if Tyler Martin hadn't put a painful wrist lock on Macy.

"That's rather unsportsmen like, old boy. Why don't you boys just take your money and go."

"Whadda yer hafta do to get a drink 'round here!" Bennington shouted.

Jack rounded the bar. "Don't I know you?"

"No. I don't believe you do." "Doc" knew who he was talking to. Macy would have too if it wasn't for his current situation.

The look in Macy's eyes might have sent some men into cardiac arrest but Tyler held and increased the pressure on Macy's wrist. Bennington started to laugh.

"Looks like you met your match, Jim. Maybe we should do what the man says and go."

Tyler let go of Macy's wrist ready for anything. Though he was still numb, Macy's intensity hadn't changed.

"If yer changed yer mind, friend, yer can take yer money and high tail it outta here. No hard feelings."

"I'll see you again."

"Do call first. Though I must say I'm not in the book."

"Come on, Macy. Let's go." Casper picked up the money on the bar and handed it to Macy. The bartender was beginning to stir as they left.

"Help me get him up, Jack." Jack brought over a chair and the two men lifted the bartender into it.

"That's it! Macy! Jim Macy! I remember now!"

18

The Storm

*E*smerelda prepared herself for what she must do, but even in her deep state of meditation she felt the ripple in the cosmic fabric of her future that coincided with the crack of the bar man's head on the floor. Her eyes were jolted open as she saw in a way only the magic of her mind's eye could see. She knew the time had come. All the players had arrived. Even in the world of Voodoo the powers she would call on were not called by many. She prayed for the strength she would need and the protection for herself and Peter.

There would be many sacrifices and blood. Peter would be with her, to help and be safe. There would be much rum and dancing, and when they were done, much sex. Sex until the rise of a new sun and a new day. It would be a new world. All the while she prayed because without the strength of God, Satan's powers could have no force. Without black there could be no white. Without good there could be no evil. It was yin and yang, each giving the other strength.

Peter had been away securing the boat. When he returned they would begin. There was no time to lose. Everything would be ready. It was ready now.

Candles burned and incense filled the back room as Esmerelda danced trancelike around the pole swinging a chicken over her head. From the altar she picked up the knife and slit its throat letting the blood drip into the carefully placed cup. Peter didn't understand the words she spoke but he knew their meanings. He watched her work the pestle mixing herbs and rum with the fresh blood.

Outside clouds gathered quickly in the western sky as the wind began to whip the water. The pressure was building its rapid tension in the air in a way that no one had seen before. I threw another anchor over hoping to get an extra hold to help the mooring line. The storm was coming fast. I wished Jack and Tyler were there to help before the storm hit, but I knew that wasn't going to happen. If I thought I had more time I would have made a run for open water. I knew I didn't. I could only hope to ride it out.

Peter watched as Esmerelda was possessed by a spirit. He was unfamiliar with it and for the first time felt afraid. He felt its power like an electric sensation on his body and all his hair stood on edge. What madness had she tapped?

Esmerelda ripped her dress open revealing portions of her flesh in its tattered remains. Grabbing another chicken she held it above her head reciting a cant in a fevered pitch before slicing off its head. Then holding it by the feet she began whipping her own body then Peter's. The blood burned his skin as it spattered. His mind became numb as he too felt possessed and began to dance. He could feel his body moving but felt he had no control over it. Even the clash of thunder seemed distance and muffled to him now. Still he moved to a rhythm he could only feel. His eyes were blinded in white light and still he danced.

Esmerelda was no longer with him but she saw it all. As if looking down from a great height. She saw Peter and she saw herself. She saw blood and she saw flesh. She saw God and Satan. And she asked them both for their help and damned them both for their interference. She was all powerful now. She would do whatever needed to be done. Nothing could stop her. Nothing could help her. It had started and would not finish till all her strength was gone and not before.

The storm blew all night. The power it unleashed would become legend in local history. In the morning the clouds swept across a magnificent blue sky. To some it may not have been a new world but to many it was definitely an altered one.

Peter awoke on the floor next to Esmerelda. Rising brought a pressure to his temples that reminded him of the frenzied events. A few of the candles still flickered, most had burnt out long ago. The room smelt of smoke and death. When he looked at Esmerelda's unmoving body, he thought she might be dead. They were both still covered in blood. On his knees by her side he shook her without a response. With his head down on her chest he could hear her heart was still beating. He lifted her in his arms. She felt light and frail and he noticed grayer then he remembered her as he placed her on their bed. First he placed a cold compress on her forehead as he ran the water in the tub. After ripping the remaining clothing from her body, he began to wipe her down with the cold cloth. The exhaustion was still with her but she began to stir.

"Yer crazy woman!" Peter felt the emotion of her coming around start to build in his throat and eyes but he fought it back.

With her eyes still shut she whispered, "It be all right now. We have mo' time."

Peter put a cool glass of water to her lips and made her drink. Then lifted her again from the bed and brought her to the soothingly cool water of the tub. He wasn't sure what she meant exactly but in time they would both feel better.

19

Omens

The storm had caught Macy and Bennington by surprise on their return trip to the "Enya". Even for a forty three foot Scarab ten to twelve foot swells in the middle of the ocean was like a cork in a child's pool filled with kids. They rode out most of the storm before the engines got flooded by a crashing wave over the stern. Then they just waited. The "Enya" was no where to be seen, at least not where she should have been.

With swells still rising to five or six feet, Macy had the back hatch open trying to dry the wires. Bennington was secretly petrified. He was looking a little green at the gills as he attempted to make the last drop of booze in his pocket last a little longer.

"Doc", see if yer can find some dry rags down below, will ya?"

"You'd think with three fuckin' engines one of them would work!" "Doc" stood up rather shakily then puked over the rail. He wiped his mouth with his sleeve before going below.

Macy laughed. "Don't worry, "Doc". We'll be going in a couple of minutes."

"That's great!" Bennington replied in a sarcastic tone as he handed Macy some towels. "And where the fuck we gonna go? There's no fuckin' boat!"

"I won't worry about that, "Doc". That oughta do it." Macy closed the hatch before cleaning his hands with one of the extra towels. ""Doc", do me a favor and get my bag. It's down below."

"Since when did I become your fuckin' servant." Casper griped as he went below. Tossing the bag onto the seat "Doc" finished the bottle he held.

"Hey, lighten up "Doc". We're still partners, remember?" Macy pulled a small electrical device from the bag. Pressing a button, Macy watched for a reaction from Bennington as he stretched out an antenna.

"What's that?" Bennington queried as he focused in.

"Call it insurance. A precautionary measure." Macy scanned the horizon with the out stretched antenna. "It's a homing device. Bring me up the charts."

Bennington went below again with no complaints.

"I activated a beeper before we left. This way we'll be able to tell if the boat drifted or the crew had made other plans."

Macy had the chart open. He had marked the exact spot where the "Enya" was when they left. The GPS aboard the Scarab gave him the location then and would pinpoint their location now. Bennington watched amazed at the accuracy. He had learned a lot about navigation on the trip up. Now this was his first encounter with modern technology.

"Look here, "Doc". This is how much we drifted since we lost our engines and the direction the currents took us. So what does that tell ya?"

"The boat should be out here somewhere." Bennington fingered an area on the chart further along the line they had drifted.

"Very good. You've learned your lessons well." The sneer in Macy's tone rattled Bennington as his hand tightened around the pistol he still had in his pocket. Macy saw the movement but went about his business, sweeping the horizon with the antenna till he picked up a faint beep.

"Ahhhh! Look's like they've been bad boys while we were away." Macy drew a line on their chart a 120 degrees from their position. "Now I'll hafta kill'em all."

When the storm hit the "Enya" its fury had the power of a hurricane. Almost immediately the swells came crashing over the deck as the wind rocked the boat from side to side. One man was lost overboard the first hour. There was no attempt to retrieve him. That was when the remaining crew took control of the boat.

Sheraton Quinn tried to lock them out of the wheel house but they managed to break their way in. Once they were in they locked Quinn and Amanda into the small storage cabin Amanda had spent the trip north in. Again it began to heat up into a stuffy sweat as the engines came up to speed. The crew was heading home.

"Dey be crazy! Macy will come and kill dem wherever dey go!" Sheraton was pacing back and forth while Amanda sat against the wall. "He'll kill dem all a thousands times over!"

"Don't look at me, this is where I came in." She sat back resting her head. "What makes you so damn sure he's even coming back?"

"He be back, I know. I see dis ship in my dreams. As a ghost ship drifting in da fog."

"You've been smokin' too much!"

"Tis da truth. And da souls of da mon he kilt, walk da decks."

"Stop it! You're giving me the creeps." Amanda got up and began to pace. "So what the hell we gonna do now?"

"Don't know, mon." He pulled two of his cigar size joints from his jacket pocket. "I don't even have any matches!"

"Maybe we should get some rest." Amanda smiled seeing the despair in Sheraton's face. She liked the man even if he didn't trust her. She couldn't blame him for that. It was part of what kept him alive. A part she understood very well.

Side by side they lay on the floor, silently staring at the ceiling. Neither said a word. Listening to the drone of the engines their minds wandered. Soon they were both asleep.

On the horizon Bennington and Macy could see the profile of the ship. The homing device had pointed them straight to her.

"How do you expect to get back on board? They know you'll kill them. They'll be ready."

Macy pulled out another device from his bag. It was smaller then the first piece of electrical equipment and seemed to consist of nothing more then a small antenna with a button.

"When we get within range, I just push the button and boom, the engine room's on fire. While they're busy with that we can get back on board."

"But that could kill Amanda."

"So what! She's half dead already. Besides, I wasn't plannin' on…"

"Well, I was! We need her!"

"What the fuck for?"

"To get Lamar outta jail for one."

"Well it ain't gonna matter. If they push the engines too hard it'll blow anyway." As the Scarab roared closer to its target black smoke began to rise from the ship. The fire bomb had gone off. Destiny had played its hand. Now the cards could only fall as they may.

If Amanda had still been sitting against the wall she would have been cut in half by the metal plate that ripped through on the explosion. Lying in each other's arms they shared the security of knowing they weren't alone. Now they shared the remaining breathable air. The room was quickly filling with smoke through the rip with nowhere else to escape either. Sheraton and Amanda crawled on their bellies to the door pounding with hands and feet for someone's help.

Smoke filled their lungs. Sheraton began to pray in words Amanda didn't understand. Amanda had lost her faith long ago. She looked at him and cried. It was the last thing she remembered before passing out. Sheraton was barely conscious when he saw the door open and two hands lift Amanda to safety.

Amanda was hacking black globs from her lungs spitting them over the rail into the sea when Sheraton came to. The morning sun had turned to a thick haze but the sea had calmed. Bennington watched them both as Sheraton sat up.

"Smokin' be bad fo your helth." He rolled back to the floor into a ball as a fit of coughing overcame him.

"Yer're lucky yer lungs are use to it or you'd be dead right now." Bennington smiled as he walked to the rail next to Amanda. After staring out to sea by her side he turned to her. "And how are you, my dear?"

She didn't respond.

Her mind wandered through a rapid series of escape scenarios. All which she knew were hopeless. Still she didn't answer, but if looks could kill.

"Ahhh! Dat be much bettar now!"

Both "Doc" and Amanda turned to look at Sheraton. Somewhere in his dazed state he found a lighter and lit one of his big cigar joints. He let out a cloud of smoke almost as big as the fire's.

When Macy returned he was carrying three gunny sacks. One held all the cash that had been on board the ship, a little under a half a million in a multitude of currencies. Inside that sack was a smaller sack with a few hand guns and ammunition. The other two sacks contained contraband. Gold and other artifacts they hadn't yet sold and drugs for pleasure and profit.

"Let's get outta here!" Macy flung the bags over the side into the Scarab.

Macy saw Sheraton heading over the side.

"Where the hell do yer think yer goin'?" Macy barked.

"He's comin' with us." Bennington said facing off against Macy with his hand deep in his pocket.

"Oh, is he? What if I just kill him now?"

"I won't do that if I were you." Bennington pulled his gun into view.

Amanda hustled over to shield Sheraton from Macy even though she knew he'd kill her just as easily.

"Go head. Pull the trigger." Macy smiled.

"I'll do it!" Casper threatened.

"I don't care if you do. I took your bullets long ago."

Bennington turned white. He pointed the gun off to the side and pulled the trigger.

Click, click, click.

Macy laughed. "Look, I don't care. Take who ever you want." With that he handed "Doc" a fully loaded semi automatic. "I'd get a holster for that. It won't fit in your pocket." Macy added dryly.

They all climbed one by one into the Scarab. Amanda sat on the back bench wrapped in a blanket next to Bennington. Sheraton watched as Macy started up the engines then lit his last joint.

"What about de others?" Quinn asked.

"There are no others." Macy replied.

As the Scarab's nose lifted from the water Sheraton looked back then nodded to Amanda to do the same. In the thundering wake the "Enya" drifted aimlessly in the ever increasing fog.

20

Changes

The ferry ride to Shelter Island would only take a few minutes. The morning had cleared into a beautiful day after the violent weather from the night before. Tyler and Jack had decided to spend the night in town even before the storm came up. That was when they ran into an old friend of Tyler'. They got to talking after a few drinks when Ralph said he was looking to sell one of his Ferraris if Tyler was interested. It was the only one in his collection that was black. It wasn't in the best condition after he had lent it to a friend who neglected the up keep. It wasn't even clean. Since then he wasn't really interested in it anymore and was willing to sell it cheap.

Tyler Martin paid half of what he knew it was worth even in the shape it was in. It was a steal at the price.

"Did all that really happen to you while you were in Rio, old boy?" The two men stood at the rail viewing blue sky and water dotted by scattered white sails on Noyack Bay. The green shore line indicted that spring had finally grabbed hold and was here to stay.

"Yeah." Jack's mind was somewhere in the past. "I never did find out what it was all about. They said leave, so I left while I had the chance."

The ferry nudged the dock and Tyler turned the key to his new toy. As bad a shape as the car might have appeared, the engine roared in the typical deep, throaty sound of a Ferrari. Enzo would be proud.

The roads on Shelter Island didn't really allow for speed. They were better suited for bicycles. Coming down the hill on Ram Island Drive, Tyler punched it a bit.

"I've always wanted one but never got around to getting one."

With the wind in his hair and blue skies above, Tyler felt like a little kid on Christmas morning. He had never been one to spend his money frivolously. Sure he spent a lot of money at any given time, but he never had anything to show for it in the end. Restaurants, hotels, bars, sure he owned several houses scattered around the world but he rarely stayed in any of them. Technically these things were in the names of his holding companies for tax purposes. Tyler rarely brought anything in his own name.

Tyler's one great gift was his ability to judge people. Those people took care of his day to day business. Their success made him even more money which he was always very generous with. His businesses were prosperous because everyone profited from their accomplishments, from top executives to cleaning people. Tyler's percentage was minimal compared to CEO's in other companies, but to him it was all profit.

"I had a Testarossa for awhile, then I lost my license, so I sold it." Jack flipped the top off a bottle of beer and downed half of it. What was on his mind was anybody's guess. Tyler's question brought it into focus.

"You said the other guy's name is Bennington? What do you suppose they're doing here, Jack?'

"I haven't the slightest idea. I just hope we don't run into them again."

"I have a feeling that's going to be inevitable. That chap, what's his name, Macy, didn't appear too happy with me." Tyler swung the car around the corner heading down the hill.

"I know. You better watch your back. I wish I had recognized them sooner."

"It won't have mattered. I had to stop him or he would have killed that guy."

"That's what worries me. He would have killed him without a second thought. He could do the same to you. That guy should have never made that bet. You never know what yer dealing with these days."

"Maybe so, old boy, but all the same, I had to…oh shit!"

Coming down off Little Ram Island the sight in front of him knotted Tyler's stomach.

Jack jumped up half way out of the car before it stopped. "What the fuck?"

There washed up on the beach was the "Nightwind". Some of her riggings had snapped and were wrapped around the mast. Tyler stopped the car in the middle of the road astounded by the spectacle of the thirty-seven foot sloop stranded on the shore. Lying on her port side in maybe a foot of water it looked twice as big as it does when in the harbor.

A car honked swerving to avoid hitting them as it sped around the bend in the road. The driver had a few choice words that were hardly audible as he raced away.

Tyler revs the engine and puts the Daytona in gear. In less than a minute they walking on the beach next to the boat.

"Do yer think…?" Jack rubbed the stubble around his mouth and chin.

"I'm sure he's alright." Tyler words weren't filled with his usual conviction.

"So…where do you think he is? It's not like him to abandon the boat."

The two men waded through the water assessing the damage. From what they could see of the hull it was intact, a few heavy scratches but nothing broken. The riggings were minor compared to what might have happen.

Suddenly the sound of a police siren filled the air. Followed by a voice through a megaphone.

"You are in a restricted area. Move away from the boat."

Tyler and Jack hadn't even noticed the yellow police tape in their rush to get to the boat. Both men headed up towards the police car when they heard through the megaphone.

"Jack? Jack Rogin?", the officer stepped from the car and headed towards the two men. "Is it really you?"

"Sam, right?" Jack wasn't really sure of the name. He did remember they played high school football together. "How are you doing?"

"I never expected to see you around here. After what happen between you and your old man. Too bad. I heard he's…"

"Excuse me, old boy. I hate to interrupt the reunion but looking for the man who was on this boat. Do you know what happen to him?" Tyler's anxiety was building.

"Sorry, Sam. He's right. We need to find out what happen to him."

"I think he might have been hurt pretty bad. Lost a lot of blood. I can't be sure. I wasn't here when they took him over to Southampton Hospital."

"Thanks, Sam. I'll catch up with you later."

Jack and Tyler were already headed to the car before Jack finished his sentence, then speed off in the direction they came in.

Sam just watched shaking his head as they left at more than twice the legal limit.

"Life is full of surprises," he thought. "I hope Jack can handle the one he's about to discover."

Luckily for Tyler they didn't run into anymore police as they put the Ferrari to the test. They made it to the hospital in record time. The emergency room was empty when they burst through the doors except for the lone overweight nurse behind the counter.

"We're looking for a friend who was brought in earlier." Tyler blurted out.

"Only family is allowed…"

"I'm his brother." Jack added but the nurse was buying it.

Tyler slipped the woman a fifty as he said, "It's very important.'

"Ok, he's back in room three down the hall. But you can't see him now. He's still with the doctor."

"Thanks." The two men were pushing through the door heading down the hall. Only Tyler made it to room three.

Jack Rogin stopped dead in his tracks as Tyler moved on. He stood in the hallway staring at the name in the slot at the first room. Rogin. After a few seconds of reading the name over and over again in his mind he stepped to the glass panel of the door to peer in. There lay his father with hoses up his nose and down his throat. He was barely breathing the oxygen that was being force into him. The IV's in his arms fed a pale white body that was hooked up to probably every machine the hospital had.

Jack stood at the door wondering what he should do. He knew the answer but still it took time to build up the courage to enter. He opened the door not knowing what to expect and went inside. He knew the old man was still alive by the steady pulse off the machines but that was the only evidence. Viewing how his father had aged since he had last seen him made Jack uneasy. He realized he never really knew the man and now was saddened by the fact that it was too late. They were different as night and day yet more alike then either of them could imagine. Silently Jack reflected how he saw his life now compared to those years gone by.

Startled, Jack's train of thought was broken as a nurse entered the room equally startled since no one else had come to see the old man.

"I'm sorry, sir. Only family members are allowed in here." The tone in her voice made Jack want to tell her to go fuck herself.

"I'm his son," was his only humble reply.

"But I was told…"

Her attitude pushed him to far.

"Well I'm back. Now get the hell outta here!" Jack yelled at her.

Cringing as she shut the door behind her, the commotion had awakened Jack Rogin senior.

"Junior. It is you, isn't it?" The old man gasped in a dry voice.

"Yeah, it's me, dad." Jack's emotion caused his words to choke.

"I'm glad you made it. It's been a long time."

"I'm afraid maybe too long. So, how you doin'?"

"They tell me I'm dying. For once I think they're right."

Jack took his father's hand in his, surprised at how frail it felt.

These were the hands that held him on his first pony ride. The hands that steadied the bike when he learned to ride. The same hands that knocked him around when he came home drunk after Betty Lou's sixteenth birthday.

There were few exchanges after that none of which made much sense. Jack felt the change from life into death as he held the hand not wanting to let go. It was too late for anything else. He left the room and informed the nurse before going to find his friends.

21

The Next Step

Esmerelda tossed and turned her way through the snake dreams for two days. On the third day she woke and ate toast and tea before falling into a deep sleep. Peter stayed by her side. On the fourth day she woke at dawn unaware of the time that had passed. She told him of her dreams. Dreams of a raging sea, a sea she controlled, she understood the power, her power but there was a strange undercurrent of which she had no control. It frightened her. In a way nothing had before. Not in a long time anyway. Only her mother's power had ever frightened her. Then she remembered, another part of the dreams. She saw her mother. Her mother was trying to warn her, only her mother was being pulled away from her by a power neither could control. Esmerelda shook with tears in her eyes as she told Peter.

"Don't worry, baby. We survived without the damn treasure this long. It ain't gonna matter if we never find it."

Esmerelda was stunned to hear Peter talk like this. Stunned yet still disbelieving.

"Go now. I be okay. Time still dominate reality. I tink everyting be okay. Go."

Peter watched as she closed her eyes falling quickly again into a deep sleep. He hadn't seen his boat in four days but he knew it was alright, he just knew. Leaving water and bread by her night stand he kissed her goodbye, then left to tend first to the guests then to his own needs.

———————

Peter sat in the cabin of his boat pondering his future. His future and Esmerelda's. He come to realize she was more then a means to an end to him. Not that he ever had really thought of her in those terms. Only now the end didn't matter as much as their survival, especially together. He was getting too old for this shit but he had been happy till this point in his life and he could live with that. He knew something was going to happen he just didn't know what.

When he returned that evening to the bed and breakfast, Esmerelda was busy making soup. Not from a can but cutting vegetables and potatoes to add to a stock she had prepared first. At first sight she stopped to put her arms around him.

"Feelin' better, eh?" Peter returned the embrace.

"I still be weak, but jes, much bettar. Tank ju for bein' dere."

"You were there fer me remember." He held her close and she closed her eyes. The rattle of the lid on the soup brought her back to her task at hand.

"How was da boat?"

"Everything's fine. I just don't know what's next."

"Well, life be full of surprises."

They had a quiet dinner with candle light and a bottle of wine at the expense of the business. Esmerelda retired early still weak from her pilgrimage through the gate.

Peter climbed the stairs to the tower hoping to find a clue. Something to show him the way. He sat reading the antique script for hours. He closed the book and rubbed his eyes. He had been facing west onto Peconic Bay. A thunder storm was building way to the west, past Riverhead. He watched the flashes of lighting light the sky then fade to a black that seemed darker then it was before. He knew it was a sensory illusion but it seemed to have a meaning that he didn't understand. Deciding he was too tired to even think about it he turned to descend the stairs.

There in the total darkness of the eastern sky was the image of a man's face, the same face he had seen before. Only now he wasn't frightened or shocked. The last few days events had numbed him plenty to such occurrences. He watched unmoving as the configuration became clearer. With a wave of its hand it seemed to be pointing into the darkness. Peter knew the points of the tower well. The direction told him Gardiners Island. Its demeanor seemed to be a warning rather then an invitation. Peter watched till it faded from sight. He stood several seconds staring into the darkness, as if he could still see it.

Again Peter opened the books to the last few pages looking for a clue to pinpoint the location. Something had to be there, it just had to.

Absentmindedly Peter began to doodle on the chart that covered the table on which he rested his books while he read. While his eyes blankly watched the book and his hand sketching the image he had seen he abruptly stopped.

"This is ridiculous!" He said aloud closing the book. "I'm gettin' nowhere fast! I can't even fuckin' draw!"

Peter turned down the lantern he used to light the tower and began to descend the stairs. Frustrated with his lack of artistic ability Peter never noticed his pencil scratches resembled a crow on a point in the chart that pointed to…

22

✦

Alive and Kickin'

"Crow Shoal." I hadn't been hurt as badly as my rescuers had originally thought.

"What are you talking about, old boy?"

"Your friend has lost a lot of blood, Mr. Martin. It would be better if he got some rest now." The doctor was annoyed about something more then the fact that Tyler had burst through the doors unannounced. Something else was on his mind.

"That's okay, Doc. I feel fine."

The doctor was pumping the blood pressure gauge with quite the unhappy look on his face. He was a seedy looking little man who needed a shave. The stethoscope around his neck made him look even shorter and was almost as cold as the look he gave me when he pressed it against my skin.

Tyler laughed at the quizzical look I gave him. I must have been a sight with the gauze bandages wrapped around my head. The doctor wasn't amused.

"Really Doc, I feel fine."

"Yes…just the same, we'll keep you here a couple more hours just to be safe." The doctor packed up his toys before saying, "I would like to have a word with you before you leave, Mr. Martin." Then he left.

"Weird little guy." Tyler said rolling his eyes. "What do you suppose he wants to talk to me about?"

I had a pretty good idea but I said, "Probably money. I don't have any remember."

"What about insurance?"

"Nope. I don't exist."

"What are you talking about, old boy?"

"I can't explain it all now. Where's Jack?"

"I don't know. He was with…"

The time had come for me to leave. I hastily threw on some clothes and headed for the window. "Meet me at the old Cedar Point Lighthouse, Jack will know where it is."

Then I slipped out the window.

"He's gone!" Both Tyler and Jack chorused as Jack entered the room. The two of them looked at each other in their own shocked disbelief. Each with different reasons and different thoughts.

The doctor confirmed what little I had told Tyler. He had checked my background for a medical history through his computer. The name existed with a fake social security number for the past fifteen years but that was about it. No licenses, no insurance, no residence, nothing. The boat was registered in the name on the I.D. but that was it.

Jack waited in the car for Tyler to return staring at a bottle of beer that was unopened.

Tyler plopped into the driver's seat. "What's going on here, Jack?"

Jack looked at him with a stern brow. "There are forces here at work beyond our control. We better move carefully." He was dead serious and Tyler knew it.

Jack kept talking as Tyler eased the car back onto the road. "It all started with that boat we saw and it ain't gonna end till we get to the bottom of it. Too many coincidences in too few days."

"I hate to say it, old boy, but I think you're right."

Silently Tyler parked the car at the end of the dirt road leading to the old lighthouse.

"We walk from here." Jack grunted as he climbed out of the car.

Neither man had spoke since they left Southampton. Jack held the bottle of now warm beer but never opened it.

Tyler had concentrated on the road. Too many unanswered questions had to wait. Each in its own time would come, he would wait. It was what he had learned, it was his way.

The walk along the beach to the lighthouse was over a mile.

"Why'd he want to meet us here?" Jack was picking up stones and tossing them in the water as they walked.

"I thought you might know, old boy."

"Haven't the slightest idea."

Tyler was carrying his shoes. "I think I'll leave these here." He had walked over to a piece of driftwood up on the dune and put them down. "I doubt anyone will bother them." They hadn't seen another soul on the beach.

Tyler asked him if he knew anything about what the doctor had told him.

"A little. You better ask him about that yourself." Jack replied in a distracted tone.

They walked a bit further before Tyler asked, "What's up, Jack?"

Jack tossed a large stone as far out as he could prior to answering. "My father died today."

"How do you know that?"

"I was there." Jack stopped in his tracks with watery eyes facing Tyler. His sorrow quickly turned to anger and he threw the still full bottle far out in to the bay screaming.

"Why? Why was I there? I just don't fuckin' understand."

"It happened there, at the hospital?" Tyler was overwhelmed.

"Yes! Don't you see! We stepped into something here. Some huge web of space and time that's controlling our world. I'm sick of it already! We need to take back our lives and fast before it's too late."

Again they walked in silence rounding the point coming into full view of the lighthouse.

"There it is."

The old lighthouse stood stoically in the sand in an area that was once its own island. Now it was a mere shell of a building sealed closed to any intrusion.

"You know, a month ago Jack, I would have thought you were crazy, but now I'm too scared to leave and more scared to stay."

"As of now, we ain't got the choice. Where the hell is he?"

Scanning the area Tyler's eye glimpsed movement at the top of the coast guard beacon tower that had replaced the lighthouse. "There he is!"

———————————

"Wait…there's no more tequila!" Jack exclaimed.

"Anyway I was thinkin' about that ship we saw. I must have fallen asleep or passed out, what ever, because when I came to everything was sideways. I figured I gotta be drunk, Then it all came back to me, everything was sideways and I was drunk. I was hoping I'd be able to get her off on the morning tide but when I stood up, I forgot there were things in places that wouldn't have normally been there. I cracked my head on something and stumbled outside just as a cop car was goin' by. They rushed me to the hospital but it's only a small cut."

"Which brings you to what I'm curious about. Jack, told me he knows a little bit about it but he said I should ask you." Tyler waited for a response with his arms folded cross his knees. Jack sat back with one elbow propped on a knee and his other leg stretched out watching the boats cruise into Sag Harbor including a forty three foot Scarab named "Quickchange".

After I scanned Northwest Harbor for a few seconds, I glanced at Jack. His eyes told me go head but I knew I would have anyway.

"I told you what happen in 'Nam."

Tyler nodded without saying a word.

"Well, after we skedaddled out of Saigon, some people seemed to think I still owed them. So I went to work for the company."

"C.I.A." Jack chimed in.

"Yeah. It wasn't bad for awhile but I began to see there was no light at the end of the tunnel. Thank god for the computer age. I wiped my total existence off. The first twenty or so years of my life. Then I faked a death. No body, no questions. I had no family left. That's what I counted on because I knew that's what they counted on."

"But how'd you do it, old boy, I mean the computers?"
"Back then nobody thought of security and I had total access. I knew more then they thought I did."

"So what's your real name?"

"I can't tell you that. If you knew it would put you in more danger than I think we're in now."

"Which brings us back to what I want know, why the hell are we here?"

"Turn around and take a look."

We all stood up and perused the horizon towards Gardiners Island. I handed Jack the binoculars I had been holding and Tyler the chart.

"See that red marker, the further one towards Cherry Hill Point."

Tyler viewed the chart then pointed.

"I know where it is." Jack's intellect reasoned quickly. "Sorry. I knew a girl over there once."

"That night when we rounded the point, that section of the island was what we saw. The rest of the island was hidden by the storm."

"Crow Shoal. There's a rock there at three feet on the low tide according to the chart." Tyler stated.

"Exactly."

"When do we start?" Jack gnarled lowering the binoculars.

23

The East End

They were a strange looking group to say the least. A short pudgy man in a baggy white sweat stained suit under a large white fedora, a skinny blonde girl in oversized men's clothes, a tall thin Rastafarian in soccer shorts and a tank top with dreadlocks all the way down his back and Jim Macy, dressed all in black with dark shades that covered his dead eyes.

The Scarab's name was "Quickchange" and after it gently nudged the dock, they blended into the madness caused by the tourists invading the east end without the slightest difference.

"So what's this brilliant plan of yours?" Macy questioned as they approached Main Street.

"Nothing so special, really. We just send Amanda here into pay the bail." Bennington was pleased with himself. Macy wasn't going to kill anybody here in broad daylight.

"And then what do we do with her?" Macy was visibly angry. "And him!"

Sheraton shot Macy a look that if anyone had even remotely expected probably wouldn't have noticed the shiver it sent down Macy's spine. Quinn was tired of Macy's threats. He was on

American soil now and didn't need the hassle, but he did still need money.

"We let'em go. We don't need'em anymore." "Doc" glanced around. His second time in America since the statutes of limitations had run out and all ready he felt at home.

"Let'em go, just like that?" In Macy's eye they were both loose ends. Loose ends that could tie too many pieces of the puzzle together.

"You won't be killin' us now, mon. Not here in A merica." Quinn's big yellow grin pissed Macy off a little more.

"People die here every day, nigger!"

"Why don't you go fuck yourself, you bastard!" It was the first time Amanda had spoken to Macy since her abduction so long ago. Macy seemed to be taken back by the outburst.

"Well, well, well. The fuckin' rag doll can talk. I was wondering when you would open your mouth for something other then my cock."

"Fuck you!" Amanda was emboldened by the sight of people around the town.

"No, fuck you, my dear." Macy could careless.

"Stop it! All of you. You're acting like children." Bennington was starting to sweat.

People were starting to take notice of this strange looking group.

"Macy, take Sheraton here and see if you can get a fix on things at the jail."

"And what the fuck are you gonna be doin'?" Macy didn't like taking orders and the throbbing vein on his forehead showed it.

"We're goin' shoppin'." "Doc" abruptly took hold of Amanda's elbow and headed into Main Street's flow of pedestrian traffic.

Macy's anger boiled as he watched Bennington walk away then turned his attention to Quinn. "What the hell are you lookin' at!"

"We need to talk, James." Quinn's face turned to a serious pose which gave him an ominous presence.

"I could still kill you now nigger!" Macy was on his toes poised like an animal ready to leap at its prey.

"I don't tink so." Quinn replied in cool tones.

As Macy began to attack Sheraton Quinn rolled his eyes into the back of their sockets. They appeared red, almost in a glowing manner. Macy doubled over in pain. His body cramped up in agony. Unable to move Sheraton towered over him.

"Dees eyes have seen fo a tao sand years, mon! I taught chu berry lit tle. I could crush chu now," Quinn clenched his fist and Macy cringed with a small moan, "but ju still owe me my money!"

Quinn released his fist and Macy fell back against the alley wall that had blocked most of this scene from the general public.

"You'll get your damned money!" Macy clutched his chest as he spoke in short breaths.

Quinn's eyes returned to their normal bloodshot appearance.

"Ju know, mon, I could really use sumting to smoke. Ju got sumting for me?"

"Yeah." Macy stood up shaking off any feelings of anxiety that still clung to him. "But first we checkout the jail house scene."

Amanda stepped from the dressing room in a skin tight black mini dress with spaghetti straps and a plunging neckline. Her feet were bare and her hair was still an unwashed stringy mess.

"Sorry dear, but you lost too much weight for that." Bennington sat sideways with his legs crossed at the ankles on a chair in the boutique. When he thought no one was looking he took a swig from the flash that had replaced the bottle in his pocket. He wasn't even sure what he was drinking anymore and it didn't matter.

Amanda wasn't happy with his comment even though she felt she looked like an old whore in the dress. "Well, what the hell are you looking for?" She snapped back standing with arms akimbo.

"I want something that will take their mind off what they're doin' while they're doin' it." With one elbow on the chair he folded one arm over the other.

"Why don't yer let me pick somethin' out. After all, that's what I used to do for a livin'."

"Okay, my dear. Go to it." "Doc" took a quick swig then returned to his waiting stance.

"Just one thing, are you really gonna let me go?"

"I got no reason to keep you, unless you want stay, but I can't guarantee what Macy might do."

"If I do what you want? Am I free?"

"Yes."

"Okay, but then I'm gone."

"Whatever you want."

Amanda turned to leave but Bennington grabbed her arm and swung her back to him.

"But if you double cross me, I'll find you and kill you myself." Amanda returned to browse the racks only thinking about a plan of escape. Assholes like Bennington didn't scare her. She'd been threatened in places where there wasn't even any law as a pretense of protection. Being in America again gave her new strength. She had grown up and lived an hour drive from where she stood now. Everything was falling into place.

An hour later when Amanda walked into the police headquarters. No one would have recognized her as the same girl that stepped off the "Quickchange". The name gave her the inspiration. From head to toe she was a different woman, it was the same way she planned to escape when the time came. Playing a part was something she did all the time in her most recent line of work. Now it would work to her advantage.

As she approached the desk the officer sitting there remained glued to the magazine he was reading, but as his eyes slowly rose from the pages they took in all of Amanda. From the high heel sandals that wrapped around her slender ankles up to her milky white thighs that seemed to continued forever till they reached the shortest pair of cut off jeans he ever recollected seeing. The hanging belt end seemed to be pointing right at her crotch. He was sure she wasn't wearing underwear. Her stomach was hard and flat, much of which was exposed under a short hot pink strapless bustier that showed enough cleavage to hold his attention momentarily. She had had her hair washed and dyed a lighter shade of blonde, it hung in long spiral curls down her back. A large pair of very dark sunglasses left her face looking beautiful yet nondescript. She was sucking on a lollipop when she asked for his help.

He sat with his mouth agape for a noticeable amount of time before he answered.

"Yes, Ma'am. What can I do for you?" Richard Hicks was a rookie officer that everyone called Dick. He hated being called Dick as much as being stuck behind the desk. He longed for the action of the streets as quiet as they were, but right this moment he was glad he was where he was.

"Well…I understand my uncle is being held here. I'd like to pay his bail and take him back to his family. They're worried sick 'bout him." She sucked on the lollipop then pulled it out of her lips smiling at the cop.

"And what would your uncle's name be, ma'am?" Dick choked on his words turning his head away in embarrassment.

"Lamar. Uncle Lamar, he's been trouble ever since mama's sister married him!" Amanda sat at the edge of the desk licking her lollipop looking all put out at the trouble this family humiliation was causing her. "I don't know why she even stays with him."

"I can't believe that unsavory character is a member of your family." Dick responded while looking through the papers on the desk.

"Remember, it's only by marriage. Will this take long?"

"Nope, I got it right here." Dick perused the sheet with widening eyes. "It's seems the charges have been dropped. He was released before I came on duty."

"Shit!" Another delay to her get away.

24

Welcome to the Real World

The storm the night before had shaken up Lamar Lorre plenty. Every bad dream he ever had in his life came back to haunt him. He hated storms even more than he hated the dark, especially if he was alone. And he was always alone. Lamar had a way about him that people would not except, not that he ever tried or cared, but he understood the way it was and accepted it. Even now, walking out of the police station a free man wasn't the normal scheme of things, though he wasn't about to stay and ask questions.

The bar owner that had pressed charges had a change of heart. It wasn't worth the effort to pursue the matter when he knew he would never receive restitution, or so he said. The barman's real attitude was not to get mixed up in something that wasn't worth more than a few hundred bucks after what had happened.

Dressed in a baggy suit that never fit right with a tie that was never pulled tight on an open collar, Lorre stepped into the brightness of a spring day. Leaves had only began to break their buds on the surrounding trees as he causally took in the whole scene around him. All was well as he headed through the alley to Main Street and headed south after crossing the road.

At the Paradise Cafe, he stopped shortly pulling a pair of sunglasses from his inside jacket pocket. As he appeared to peer into the window he noticed two men that he had noticed when he left the jail. Again he crossed the street, now heading north, he didn't stop until he reached Schooners then went in.

He took a stand at the far side of the bar so he could watch the door. His suspicions were right. The two men passed the doorway then began to mill around the windows till one of them entered the bar.

Lamar hoped he had the advantage. He knew the terrain and he had never seen this jamoca in the black shades before.

"Bill, ask my friend here what he'll have?"

Macy turned colder then artic ice. "I don't know you, do I, pal?"

"Oh, I though we were close. It appears I was wrong."

Lamar headed for the back entrance, the steps up the alley would take him back towards the police station. But fate played its hand.

"Lamar!"

At the top of the stairs stood Peter Winthorpe. Lamar owed him and Esmerelda a good deal of money.

"Lamar! You bastard! Get back here!" Peter took off down the stairs as Lorre knocked Macy back into the rear gateway at Schooners. Peter was hot in pursuit not noticing the man in the dark shades he passed.

Lamar shot out the alley right into the street where he was knocked to the ground by a speeding police car who put his lights on after the impact. The county cop immediately pulled his weapon as he approached the downed man.

Peter stopped in his tracks as did Macy. Lamar laid on the tarmac with blood oozing from his orifices. The tourists began to gather around this macabre scene. Peter changed directions knowing he would never see that money now. He didn't notice Macy standing at the street's alley entrance, but Macy noticed him.

"I guess we don't need the weasel anymore." Macy thought to himself.

Quinn came along side having witnessed the action from another point of view.

"What happon, mon?"

"Nothing to do with us. Let's get the hell outta here."

Macy and Quinn walked to the wharf. It was just a feeling Macy had after seeing Winthorpe. He blew it when he didn't follow him immediately, he knew that. He was getting old, but when Lamar got run down his mind went blank. He was tired of all the cat and mouse games, but it wasn't over yet. He spotted Winthorpe heading to the channel in an old scow named "Dreamtime".

"Ju know, da mon dat come from de alley aftar da mon we wont look berry familiar to me."

"How the hell would you know…"

"Didn't say I know, I say he look familiar. Look like da mon dat disappear wiff my sister." Quinn watched the waters as the boats came and went. "Dat be a long time ago. I can't be sure."

"Let's get to the boat. I want to take a spin."

____

"He's gone!"

"Whadda yer mean he's gone?"

"He's gone! They let him go!" Amanda was pissed. There was no way out of the back of the jail.

"Where'd he go?"

"How the fuck should I know!" She wanted out but kept running into dead ends.

"Well, it wasn't that long ago. Maybe he's still around town somewhere."

Amanda didn't say a word. She went down the stairs that led to the street between Schooners and the firehouse into the crowd that still gathered on the street. The ambulance's lights flashed brighter than the afternoon sun.

"What the hell's goin' on here?" "Doc" question unaware of what had happened.

Amanda nudged her way through the crowd but didn't recognize the face she observed being put into the back of the rescue vehicle. She slowly made her way back to Bennington looking for a possible way to escape.

"It wasn't Macy, was it?" Bennington said dryly.

"No such luck."

"Too bad. Let's just head back to the boat. Maybe, he came up with something."

"Yeah, right, great." Amanda was an unhappy camper, a fact that didn't slip by Casper Bennington.

———————

When they reached the slip the boat was gone. Off in the far distance they could see it motoring through the harbor with Macy at the wheel. A large almost transparent cloud rose over Sheraton Quinn before quickly dispersing in the air.

"Looks like we missed the boat, dear."

"Where the hell they goin'?"

"Don't worry, my dear. They'll be back."

Amanda looked at Bennington with unequivocal disgust in her eyes. Escape seemed to be escaping her as time passed. The tone in her voice was obvious.

"And what the hell makes you so sure?"

"Macy, ain't goin' nowhere without this." Bennington pulled a small black book from his pocket holding it triumphantly in the air. "Whadda you say we get an early dinner, my treat." Bennington reminded her in his subtle way that he was still in control.

25

❧

Tides They Are
A Changin'

"Ju not be a tractin too much tention." Sheraton sat in the copilot seat smoking a joint laughing.

"Well, what the hell do you expect me to do, run by him ten times till he knows our numbers by heart?" Macy knew they were attracting attention. A Scarab traveling as slow as they were was bound to be noticed.

"Shit! Ju coulda went 'round da island tree times already."

"You got the damn chart? Where's he headed?" Macy was getting more annoyed every second.

"If he be goin' in dere, dat be Coc kills Harbor." Quinn watched as he sucked down the last of the joint he held.

"Let me see." Macy took the chart.

"Right dere." Sheraton pointed.

"One way in, one way out."

"Dat right, mon."

"Okay, we wait." Macy cut the engines. The boat slowly continued to the west but the slight current held it till the boat turned then lazily started to drift east.

Macy pulled a pair of binoculars from under the seat that could see a fly on a cow's ass half a mile away. He passed them over to Quinn.

"He's rounding that point."

"Hmm, so what now, boss?" Quinn smiled as he handed the binoculars back to Macy. Macy didn't even notice the dig.

"We get a little closer." Macy had his eyes glued to the magnifiers.

"Who da hell is he?"

"He's the reason we're here!"

On the harbor side of the roadway opposite Lower Beach, the "Nightwind" sat between fifteen and twenty degrees on her port side. The tide was about as high as it was going to get without a storm surge to push it past its max. We were ready waiting for the captain of the boat Jack and Tyler hired on short notice.

After they retrieved Tyler's car they headed into Sag Harbor before taking the boat across to Shelter Island. In a small bar near the eastern edge of the marina they ran into a guy who was telling the bartender how a guy that owed him money just got hit by a car.

"A damn police car, no less! Now I'll never see the money!"

"That's too bad, Pete."

"Damn right it is! I need money to run the boat."

"Pardon me, old boy." Tyler interjected. "I couldn't help but over hear, you have a boat and need money. We just so happen to need a little maritime assistance and are willing to negotiate a price."

"Nothing legal, I hope." Peter sat up smiling with his beer still in hand. "Let's hear what yer have to say."

"Nothing so romantic." Jack quipped, still in a somber mood since earlier with good reason.

"We're hoping we just need a little muscle in the way of a tow. Nothing to drastic."

Peter Winthorpe's eyes lit up though his poker face didn't show it when they named a price. He hedged and hawed till they offered a little more, then he took it. Half now, the rest when he showed. They knew they overpaid but time was more important. He said he'd be there on the tide. They left and he followed.

Now we waited as he came into view. Each one of us hoped the tide had raised her enough to pull her from the beach. Secretly each one of us doubted it. We had to give it a try now or wait till the next tide, which probably wouldn't yield very different results.

Within the next fifteen minutes, Winthorpe had "Dreamtime" pointed to deeper water as we strung a heavy line around the hull of the "Nightwind". Before tying it off on the stern cleats of the motor boat, we tied a few life jackets to the line to protect the hull of the beached boat and keep the line high up on the waterline. This wasn't the best way of doing this but we were improvising in our race with the tide. The longer she sat on the beach rising and falling on the tide, the more chance she would sustain serious damage.

Putting on my snorkel gear I entered the water as Winthorpe began a futile attempt to free my boat.

"Whoa! Whoa! Whoa!" Shouting above the roar of the engine and churning waters after I broke the surface Winthorpe cut the power.

"It's no good." I lamented.

"Maybe if I had the sheer energy of a beast like that!" Winthorpe pointed to the large Scarab that drifted a few hundred yards directly in front of his bow.

"No, that's not the problem. The keel's digging in. She's not high enough. We gotta force her to heel more."

"How do you prescribe we do that, old boy?"

"I know!" Jack shouted.

Using the halyard from the mainsheet with added line for more length, we tied one end to the chassis of Tyler's car for an anchor. Jack was on board using the winch to pull her over onto the gunwale. Luckily the riggings that were taking the strain hadn't been damaged.

As the sea water was about to enter my boat I checked the position of the keel on the bottom.

"She should come off!" I yelled to Winthorpe who had already started his engine. "Ease her off slow."

Jack started to release the line as the "Nightwind" started to inch back into the water. Winthorpe had his engine going strong. Suddenly the line that was attached to the Ferrari snapped. Jack fell to the deck as the boat lurched into the deeper water. Fortuitously Peter Winthorpe was fully aware of the quick change and swung his boat hard to port. The "Nightwind" shot past him in its uncontrolled drift. A collision had been avoided but in the second that passed of slack time in the line it managed to wrap around the propeller shaft of "Dreamtime." When the line pulled taught again, it swung both boats like dancing partners. Everyone heard the strained pull of the steel shaft as it reverberated through the water.

"Dreamtime" stopped dead in the water. The bend in the shaft caused her to throw a bearing. Her engine couldn't turn.

"Shit! Now I'm totally fucked!" Peter threw his cap. It was the first available thing in reach.

"Don't worry, old boy. I cover whatever the damages are." Tyler shouted from the shore.

"That's fuckin' great. This damn boat's so old I don't even know if I can get her fixed."

"I'll see that it's taken care of. Just give me a couple of days."

"Yeah. If Tyler says it, you can be sure it'll be done. Better then new." Jack joined in rubbing his sore areas from the fall.

"A couple of days!? I'm fucked. Time is the one thing I don't have."

"Don't worry, I'll pay you for your time too, old boy."

"Right. You're gonna pay me. Pay for my boat, and pay for my time." Peter was in a state of disgust. "You couldn't afford me if you were a millionaire!"

"Actually, Pete. He could afford you if you were a millionaire." Jack groaned as he rubbed a sore spot on his elbow. "I need a beer!"

The Scarab drifted more on the current of the tide that had already started to ebb then the slight breeze that rippled the water from its mirror image. Macy and Quinn had watched the whole scene without a word said between them.

Finally Macy put down the binoculars. "That guy looks familiar."

Quinn laughed. "Yeah, mon. We be followin' him, remember?"

Macy sneered at him with a smirk. "Not him, the other guy. The one in the water with the mask." Macy handed Quinn the glasses again.

"Don't know, mon."

"Well, I do." Macy took them back. "It'll come to me. It don't matter though. The others are gonna die, he might as well go with'em."

He had recognized Tyler and Jack from the bar. He had previously promised himself he would kill Tyler when their paths crossed again, as he did with Jack and Winthorpe many years ago. The coincidence that they were all together never even occurred to him. And he hadn't even recognized me yet.

26

Girlfriends

The season was in full swing but the tables on the back patio were starting to empty out from the late lunch crowd. Amanda and Bennington took a seat in the back corner away from the flow of pedestrian traffic. Still dressed in her "bail at the jail" outfit, Amanda looking around her surroundings was hopeful at the possibilities. Bennington was dressed as usual only he was more noticeably dingy in appearance on this side of the equator.

After a while a waiter came over and told them they would only be able to order drinks and appetizers.

"The kitchen closes while they prepare for dinner." The waiter was obviously resentful at having to work during this slow period.

"Then how the hell can we get appetizers?" Amanda's mood was like that of a spoiled brat that wasn't getting her way. The fact that they couldn't get food had nothing to do with it.

"Just bring us one of each for now. And a Jack Daniel's straight up. In fact make it a double. And for you, my dear?" Bennington turned his attention from the waiter, who could care less if they stayed or left, to the blonde at his side with the never ending expanse of thighs. "Adonis is waiting, my dear."

That brought a smile she couldn't conceal and a more annoyed attitude from their waiter. "Jack Daniel's, huh? I'll have the same." Amanda said then flicked her hand to send the boy off.

"Oh, you're bad, Amanda. That's what I always liked about you."

"It's the only side of me you have ever known." Amanda's emotions had started to boil at the realization of being in the U.S. She knew this place and liked it. She was here to stay and nothing was going to stop her.

"That's probably true. We could start all…"

"Would you mind if I went to the lady's room first?"

"Why not." Then he changed from a jovial tone to one of pure malice. "I'll wait for you in the bar."

Bennington knew the women's room entrance was right off one side of the bar. Macy and him had stopped here on their search for Lamar. After making sure she went where she said she was going he took a seat at the bar with a good view of the door.

There was no other way out then the way she came in. Now she was not so sure her scheme would work but she began to carry out her plan anyway. From her large shoulder bag she pulled the scissors she stole from the hair salon and began cutting. When she had hacked enough off to pass for a boy she reached for the black dye she also grabbed. Amanda had been busy shoplifting all afternoon.

So far, no one else had entered the restroom. Which was good and bad. She had been alone while she worked on her hair, but she needed more bodies to help cover her tracks when she left. After drying her hair as best she could with paper towels and the bathroom hand dryer, she went into a stall. She had taken an off white calico dress and a pair of sandals from the shop "Doc" had bought the rest of her outfit. The dress was a little large and covered her frail frame more the adequately.

Again she stood peering into the mirror. The change was remarkable. She had combed her hair so it was plastered to her head which made her look smaller.

Just then a group of five to six girls entered the room, she wasn't sure in the confusion. Amanda busied herself at the mirror as one of the girls took up a position next to her. The sweet little thing needed to fix her make up.

Amanda eyed her with envy. She could remember when she was that young, with firm breasts and taunt muscles, without the hint of a wrinkle on her face. The thoughts of this girl's young body began to excite Amanda but her main concern brought her mind back into focus.

"Could I borrow your eyeliner for a moment, Sweetie?" Amanda smiled like she hadn't smiled in a long time. This girl excited her. So what was wrong with mixing business and pleasure. The girl smiled back and actually blushed a little. Amanda was still a fine looking woman even though she was older then the girl who stood next to her. In fact, Amanda was a damn good looking woman for her age, no matter who was standing next to her.

"Sure, but I don't think you really need it." The younger beauty handed over the pencil.

"Maybe not, but you never know." Amanda then proceeded to put a small dot slightly higher then her lips on the right side of her face.

————

Bennington sat on a stool at the bar growing steadily more impatient. Amanda seemed to have been gone a long time when in fact it had only been about ten minutes. It was about that time that he began to pick up a conversation the bartender was having with another patron.

"Yeah, really. It was right out here in front. He ran right into a police car."

"No shit!" The customer raised his glass. "It couldn'ta happen to a nicer guy. I think he owed ninety percent of the town money."

"Well, it don't look like they're gonna get it now."

"Maybe not, but that bastard still had it coming."

"If you say so, but anyone who extended Lamar credit took that risk on their own. Nobody forced them."

"That don't make it right."

When the group of young giggling girls entered the bar the conversation stopped. Bennington's mind was occupied on what he heard. He temporarily lost track of time as the girls came and went from the door he had been watching. He never noticed Amanda leave with the girl she befriended in the lady's room. With dark rose oval shaped wire rimmed glasses Amanda glanced over her shoulder as she left the bar with Courtney.

Courtney was shorter then Amanda with dark brown hair cut stylishly to her shoulders. Her bright blue eyes were all that distracted your attention from her smile. Courtney had a room two doors from Schooners. The two of them disappeared from the street in seconds. By the time Bennington realized no one was left in the lady's room it was too late. Amanda was gone.

———————

After about two hours or more of twisting bodies and the exchange of tongues in various spots, both girls had reached their ultimate goal. Many times. Amanda lay on her side with her breasts pressed tight against young Courtney's back. The slow rhythm of her hips still rubbed her pubic hair against the younger woman's buttocks.

Now Amanda lay awake feeling guilty as the other girl slept. Not about the sex but the thought of possibly having involved this young girl in any danger because of her escape. She gently stroked Courtney's stomach and breasts. She knew she had to leave but didn't want to. She was happy here.

Amanda slowly pulled away from Courtney kissing the nape of her next as she did. She had originally thought of taking her money when she left but she knew she couldn't do that now. She loved this girl and was sorry. She would slip into the darkness of the night that had fallen and not risk or endanger this girl again.

For that, she was even more sadden.

Walking down Main Street Amanda's eyes were filled with tears as she ran into the black woman coming out the front door of the Paradise Cafe. The cafe had been closed for hours and was quite dark at this time in the evening.

"Sorry, child. It be my fault" Esmerelda had been making a delivery of the muffins she had baked for the breakfast crowd. She had the key and always delivered the freshly baked goods the night before.

"I'm sorry, I wasn't lookin'…"

"Dat be okay. What be the mattar, child?"

Amanda started to cry like the dam had broken. All her emotions had exploded on this kind face. One that had looked so familiar though she had never known.

"Jest come wiff me child. Ju be safe."

Amanda walked with the woman into the dark. They seemed to disappear into the night leaving the world behind. Amanda felt safe in this darkness, as if she were under the wing of her guardian angel.

27

※

Strange Bedfellas

After having anchored the wounded "Nightwind", we tied Winthorpe's "Dreamtime" to one of my rear cleats letting her sway in the breeze. The two crippled vessels hung onto each other with nowhere else to go as Tyler counted out the rest of the money he promised.

"Here's an extra fifty for all the trouble we caused you, old boy. And don't worry I'll get your boat fixed."

"I dun't have much choice, do I, but I thank ya all the same." Peter extended a hand which Tyler gladly shook.

Jack had pulled an ice chest full of Coronas from the Ferrari and was busy handing them out. I took one while I busied myself checking the damage to my boat. There was something about Winthorpe that didn't sit right with me, so I wasn't that anxious to get involved.

"So what's the big rush, I mean, why the race against time with the boat?" Jack plopped down with a second beer in his hand that he was opening.

"Ya'll understand if I don't answer."

119

Jack looked out to the west as the slightest breeze blew from the north. Twilight had past its peak turning to deep purples with the hint of orange on the horizon.

"Sure, old boy. We all got skeletons in the closet." Tyler interjected to keep the conversation going as he eyed me.

"Yer accent ain't 'xactly British, is it?"

"No, it isn't. I was born here. Boston actually." Tyler went on to explain the heritage of his English ways.

"Where exactly are you boys from?" Peter questioned.

"We were down in Key West…" Jack burst in telling Peter in his most flamboyant terms of our experiences. When Jack handed Peter another beer during this tale of high adventure, it finally hit Peter that 'dere were tree of us'.

Winthorpe couldn't help but laugh at Jack's exaggerated anecdotes. Even I was laughing and I had been there. Jack was so involved in entertaining Winthorpe he didn't notice the change in his expression when he mentioned the ship we saw in that first storm. Tyler and I did though.

"So why exactly did you boys come here?" Winthorpe was to the point without any kind of roundabout concern, like as to why we left Key West in the first place.

"I had a job with the inn." I thumbed the direction over my shoulder. "Or so I thought." Now I was much more concerned as to our involvement with Peter Winthorpe.

"Oh. So did I. Bloody bastard." Winthorpe slugged down the rest of his bottle then threw it at the inn. We all heard the splash and waited for his explanation. "Used to sell'em fresh fish, at a good price too. They say the new owner's got connections. Mafia. I don't know fer sure. I don't get involved. I sure do miss the money, though."

Jack handed Winthorpe another beer, in fact we all took one. Tyler had his head tilted back looking at the emerging stars when suddenly it shot forward. With a wide smile across his face he made sure he had my attention before he started talking. I held up a forefinger before he started to speak and quickly lit all the lanterns that had ample material to stay lit.

The only sound during that time was Jack opening another beer for himself and the creak of the lines holding the boats.

"Ya know, Jack and I spent the day at the library trying to find out what we could about that ship we saw." Tyler could tell by the look on Jack's face that the fuse had been ignited. "What we needed to know most…"

"Was out…by a guy named…Winthorpe!"

"Bingo!" Tyler raised a bottle to Jack and I as Winthorpe appeared to be in a dazed state of deep thought.

"It seems fate has drawn us together." I mused probably as piqued by the fact as he was.

"There might be more to that then yer know." Peter scratched his head with his left hand underneath his cap then fixed its position on his head. He was thinking of Esmerelda and her mystic sorcery. Things certainly had taken a strange turn of events. The question was, was he ready to walk the tightrope and risk it all or trust the net for dubious glory?

———————

"This is a nice little place you have here." Amanda had just received the grand tour. "Just you and your husband run it?"

"Dat's right. We be heir a while now. We do alright."

"It's nice. I like it."

"I like it, too." Esmerelda smiled a wide grin. She was proud of the business she had established on this little island. "Dere be a small cabin in da back. Passed da chickens. It is not much but ju r welcum to stay."

"Okay, but only if there's somethin' I can do to help you around here."

"Child, dere is always somethin' to do 'round here." Both women laughed as Esmerelda led Amanda to the shack out back.

———————

"So, tell me what yers saw."

Jack started but Tyler immediately interrupted. "Not so fast, Jack. Why don't you tell us what you know first," he said looking right at Winthorpe.

Peter Winthorpe rubbed a couple of days growth of his chin then took another swig of beer before looking at the bottle. Obviously, he was weighing his options, something Tyler's mind had already done.

"Well, her name was the "Corona", a whaler whose home port was Sag Harbor. She also done a little pirating, from what I gathered." Peter was holding his cards close to his chest.

Jack watched as Tyler walked over to get another beer. I waited because I wasn't sure what his next move would be.

"Why are you looking for her, old boy?"

"Historic value." Winthorpe didn't like Tyler, only his money. It was becoming blatantly apparent.

"Bullshit! You don't know where she went down and we do." Tyler let that sink in before adding. "So tell us more and we can cut a deal."

Impressed as I was with Tyler's tactics, telling him what he wanted to know without telling him nothing, I wasn't sure it would work with a guy like Winthorpe. I was more then surprised when he started talking.

"Back in 1518 Cortez was sent to Mexico after helpin' Velasquez take over Cuba. After Mexico Valasquez had wanted him to come back to Cuba so he burnt all his ships to make sure no one could leave. Then Cortez wipes out all the tribes along the coast before heading inland to where the chief of the Aztecs held court." Jack handed Winthopre another beer noting his bottle had long been empty.

"Anyway, he gets there 'xpectin' a fight. Instead Montezuma, the king or whatever the fuck he calls himself, greets him with open arms. Thinks he's some sort of fuckin' god or somethin', because he's white. Showers him with presents, one of which is a dagger. Solid gold with a jewel encrusted handle."

"I never read squat about this, old boy."

"No one did, because the dagger never made it out of Mexico." Winthorpe takes a long drink on his bottle of beer. He must have been getting thirsty. He was definitely getting excited by his own tale. "Montezuma's people already hated him. They hated Cortez. When Cortez finds out they're plannin' to kill him, he takes Montezuma hostage but Montezuma ends up gettin' killed by his own people, no less."

"This story's startin' to sound familiar." Jack quips looking at me.

"Cortez runs with nowhere to go really. Ends up on the Yucatan at Chichen Itza where he hides it among the pyramids."

"The dagger?" Jack interrupts.

"Yeah. So in 1521, Cortez recaptures Mexico City and settles in. He sends some troops to the pyramids to recover it."

"The dagger?" Jack questions again.

"Right." Winthorpe eyes Jack not quite sure what to make of him. "But, they can't find it."

"But you did." Tyler interjected seemingly disbelieving what he had heard so far.

"I didn't say that, did I. old boy." Winthorpe's mocking Tyler didn't pass unnoticed by anyone, but Tyler let it slide as long as Winthorpe kept talking. "At that point things get cloudy. Local legends say the Aztecs found it after Cortez ran. It was passed among their royal families durin' their decline and used as the weapon of choice for royal advancement by assassination."

"That's quite a story, Peter, old boy, but how do you come to know all this?"

"If yer let me finish ya'll find out."

From where I sat, I think Tyler pushed him just enough to tell us everything.

"They say the dagger carries a curse to anyone who seeks to possess it. Anyone who has had it died because of it."

"Well, it was a couple a hundred years ago." Jack joked.

"Don't take it lightly, friend!" Winthorpe's tone had changed.

He was a man who believed in the powers from whatever source. His face grew very serious. "Anyone who ever owned the dagger died by it or because of it. The only one who didn't was Cortez. And he never really held it in his possession."

There was silence now as we listened to the night and the water lapping against the hulls of the boats.

"So, what happened next?" I queried before Peter stopped talking for good.

"Somewhere along the line someone decides to rid himself of the curse and places the dagger back at the ruins." Winthorpe finishes off his beer and gets up for another one which Jack is already handing him. Standing with one arm leaning on the boom, he continues, "It lays there untouched for two hundred years, till some grave robbers find it. They decide to sell it but don't find a buyer right away. They end up killing each other but the dagger bounces around on the open market before some plunderers stumble upon it. The one in particular that happen to receive it as a reward for saving the ship's captain was a relative of mine."

Silence hung as heavy as the darkness in the new moon. We waited till Jack finally asked the question.

"But what does that have to do with the ship we saw?"

"That was the ship he was workin' when it got lost again."

"So you think it went down with the boat?" I questioned before Jack was able to gather his thoughts.

"I'm really not sure." Peter replied. "But that's where the trail ends. And that's a hundred and fifty years ago."

28

Mad Dog

pon returning to their transitional slip, Macy and Sheraton found Bennington sitting on a bench alone. His legs were crossed and his hands rested on a cane that he had acquired somewhere along the way. Even from a short distance "Doc" appeared to be watching the sunset that had long vanished but Casper Bennington was passed out cold.

After Macy got tired of eyeballing the drudgery of ship salvage, he gunned the engines leaving a temporary hole in the water. His quick action sent Sheraton stumbling for a grasp to steady himself. Macy just laughed.

"What da hell is wrung with ju, mon!"

"Just bored! Looks like they'll be there awhile." Macy was having a hard time seeing over the bow of the boat till it began to plane off. His five foot five and three quarters inch frame appeared to be even smaller at the helm of the forty-three foot boat.

They were tying up in Sag Harbor within ten minutes.

"She musta broke his heart." Macy said with a sneer as he eyed Bennington.

Sitting beside "Doc" on the bench Sheraton shook him with no response other then the collapse of his hands from the cane.

"Come on, help me get him in the boat." Macy was peeved at having to babysit Bennington especially after he let Amanda get away. He would rather have left him there but he didn't need to attract the attention. Besides he still needed "Doc's" expertise in antiquities. Macy pulled Bennington up by his left arm swinging the arm around his neck as Sheraton retrieved the cane then help support him on the right.

Once on board they threw him into a sleeping bunk where Bennington moaned then rolled over and began to snore. Macy went to a storage cabin pulled out a black bag and a black windbreaker. With his back to Sheraton he began to stuff the pockets with items from the bag. Sheraton watched but couldn't see what he was doing. Then Macy put the bag away before approaching Quinn who had taken a seat.

"Here," Macy handed him two joints, "keep an eye on the buzzsaw. I'll be back in a little while."

"And what if dere's a problem?" Sheraton pointed at Bennington with the two joints in his hand.

"Don't worry 'bout him. He'll be out till I get back. Just remember, that shit's illegal round here. So don't be so open about it."

"Got chu, mon."

Macy left the boat slipping into the darkness of the night. Sheraton observed the scene as he lit up, then watched as a cloud of smoke disappeared in the same manner.

The first plan of action Macy pursued was to head back to Shelter Island. After hot wiring a car, some non descript little shitbox whose make had no concern to him, he found his way back to the spot he had left earlier in the Scarab. Both boats were deserted. Macy decided it wasn't worth waiting around. He knew they would both be back in the morning. So he turned the car around and headed back to Sag Harbor.

The roads were dark and Macy was traveling slow. His mind was drifting among the thoughts of the last twenty four hours. The one thought that kept coming back was Amanda, he was horny and she was gone. Unless Bennington had given her money, which he doubted, she had to be somewhere in the area. She couldn't have gotten far. Bennington's fantasy was that she would stay with him. No one could have believed that but him.

Once the ferry returned to Long Island Macy began to stop at every bar he saw figuring if she was looking to make money she would pick up on the occupation she knew so well. With no luck after about a dozen or so places, he was starting to get surly. He was pushing to get into a fight if he couldn't get laid.

In a tiny dive on the outskirts of town he met Betty. She was a local who was always out on the prowl. Her husband drove big rigs cross country but even when he was there he didn't pay much attention to her unless he wanted something. She always wanted something and was hot on Macy as soon as he entered the bar. Betty wasn't too bad looking to Macy who had had enough not to really notice or care.

After a few drinks they headed out to a motel but decided the back seat was as good a place as any. The car rocked as the windows steamed up. Macy stroked harder and harder into Betty who was on all fours. Faster and faster the motion increased. She heard the click as she started to come then Macy grabbed her hair pulling her head back and slit her throat with the switchblade. As her body convulsed, he continued to pound into her till he was spent.

———————————

Sheraton sat on the back bench of "Quickchange" looking over the port side at the lights of Sag Harbor only a few blocks away. He took a long drag on the second joint. Macy had been gone quite awhile now, but somehow Sheraton knew he would be coming back. He smoked off the rest of the joint then sucked it in and chewed it up watching and listening to the sounds of the town.

"Merica ain't what I be 'xpectin'." Quinn mumbled to himself. Just then he heard a grunt and moan from Bennington so he thought he better go check on him. Sheraton couldn't help but laugh, Bennington had fallen off the bed. At least part of him had. His feet were still on the bunk but the rest of him was crumpled headfirst between the benches fast asleep. His stained white suit jacket was twisted all around him.

Sheraton pulled his feet off the bunk and placed them on the floor. He wasn't going to try to lift this pudgy little man by himself. Bennington's coat was still wrapped around his torso so Quinn decided he better remove it so the old man could breathe. He rolled "Doc" to one side then the other pulling the sleeves from his arms without the slightest sign of disturbing him.

Quinn folded the jacket and was about to toss it on the bed when he felt the black book in the side pocket. Pulling it from the pocket he absentmindedly placed the garment down on the bench above Bennington. Sheraton knew right away that the book belonged to Macy. Not because of the pirate like skull and crossbones on the cover, but by the VooDoo marks that surrounded it. He had no idea what Bennington was doing with it.

Carefully opening the small book Quinn wasn't quite sure what he was looking at. In it were names and dates. In some of the places where a name would usually appear, unknown was written. Some names didn't have dates after them. He flipped through the pages figuring there were a hundred or so entries. Then he went back to the beginning. The dates written started right before Macy and Bennington had taken over the ship. He flipped to the latter pages where he recognized the names of some of the men on the "Enya" including his own. They all had the same date, his was blank.

Sheraton closed the book looking at Bennington wasted on the floor. He was pretty sure he knew what he was looking at now. It was a death list. Sheraton flipped through the pages again.

"Dis be one bad muddafucka." Quinn thought sitting back stretching his long legs over Bennington from bench to bench. He began perusing through the names at the start of the book when he came upon the name Peter Winthorpe. There was no date after Winthorpe's name or after the unknown slot that followed.

Sheraton hadn't thought of that name in fifteen years. Not since he was a small boy and his sister left the island with a man by that name. How many could there be? And now that he was thinking of her why did he have an overwhelming sensation she was near by?

———

Macy parked the car on a deserted dead end street less then half a mile from the marina. The lump of flesh that was once Betty Halsey lay slumped in the back seat. Most of the blood from the body had soaked into the seat and floor mats.

Driving to the end of the block with the lights off, Macy locked the door when he left then pulled a device from his pocket. In the total darkness that surrounded him he twisted a dial then crouched down and put the mechanism next to the gas tank.

By the time he walked to the end of the block a small explosion occurred starting an intense small fire under the automobile. In less time then that Macy had totally disappeared into the night when the tank exploded and the car was engulfed in flames.

Only the whispers of a slow cool voice that nobody heard in the darkness broke the stillness of the night.

"Yeah! She's one hot babe."

———

Sheraton looked at the book in his left hand under the darkness of starlight. He scratched his head with his right hand then pulled another joint from his shirt pocket. He had found Macy's stash a long time ago and wasn't about to be fed his small pittance at Macy's whim. He lit the joint that was triple in size to those Macy had given him and leaned back with the book still in his hand.

Quinn's eyes rolled into the back of his head as he looked at the world from the dark side.

Death was a way of life. Macy thought he knew the dark side. Only while he may have felt he controlled it, it controlled him. It used him as its tool. An instrument played for its amusement. Like a puppet controlled by the hand of fate.

Sheraton saw with the eyes of the power within himself. The power of the book felt through fingers that sensed the evil it held. Powerful enough to destroy or control.

Sheraton knew his needs and knew he should hold unto this tidbit of information, for in the long run he knew everything mattered when it came to the power.

29

❧

Going Home

Tyler and I sat on the front porch of the Duval Cafe sipping at a bottle of Long Island white wine, I'm not sure which, waiting for the appetizers to arrive. Years ago this old building had been a Bohack's but was most recently used for the food service industry. The night was quiet and the ambience fit the mood with the sounds of an old scratchy recording from the early thirties.

"So what do you think of his story, old boy?" Tyler suddenly asked putting his glass down. The dim light of the candles showed his face looking older as his thoughts etched themselves into his features.

"If you mean do I think he's tellin' the truth, I would say yes. If I think he's told us everything I'd say no."

"Yeah, me too." Tyler picked up his glass again after I refilled it with the cold wine. "What do you think about the curse?"

"Not much. Curses have a way of formulating after the fact. After all, like Jack said they'd all be dead anyway."

"Where'd Jack go? He asked to borrow my car. I said I'd take him but he said he had to go alone."

"He was goin' to his old man's wake. I told him we'd come but he said no. He had to do it by himself." I replied after taking a sip of the cool wine.

The waitress brought the appetizers which we began to devour right away. The conversation was momentarily interrupted while we quickly started to consume the food.

"Tyler, you don't like him very much, do ya?"

"I assume you mean Winthorpe."

"Of course."

"Actually, I'm not sure."

"Well, he doesn't seem to like you!"

"It might just be the situation, old boy. I'm sure he wasn't planning to share the profits."

"So why do ya think he was so willin' to talk right away?"

"That's a good question, one I've been thinking about myself."

"So tell me something else, what do ya think it all has to do with us? I mean why do you think we saw the damn thing in the first place?"

"It is all rather odd, isn't it. First the apparition, then Jack and I happen to be in the bar with the guys Jack ran into in South America. You tell us a story and all the people who happen to be in that ominous tale are now dead, by dubious circumstances. Jack's father dies and he just happens to be there after not seeing him for years."

"Jack's got a few other stories he might wanna tell ya someday, but whadda ya think?"

"I don't know, old boy. I thought you guys were the experts on this sort of thing." Tyler seemed a little pissed then took a long sip of the wine before offering his glass for refill with a pause. "Sorry. I'm not quite sure what's eating me."

I let the silence take over the air before I began.

"Think about it. Jack ran into these guys and it involved antiquities of value, shall we say."

"Okay."

"Jack's father dies."

"So you're saying it revolves around Jack, old boy."

"No, I'm not. Chances are Winthorpe had a run in with these guys, too."

"How do you figure that?"

"Pure speculation, but Winthorpe is looking for something in their market. Old and valuable. And wasn't it something to do with antiquities in South America."

"Good point, but all the same, it could just as well revolve around you, old boy."

"How do you figure that?"

"Like I said, we all have our skeletons in the closet."

"Well, we know mine. What are yours?"

Jack sat outside the funeral home at a distance with the top down on the Ferrari watching the people enter the building. He only recognized a few out of the crowd. His father's lawyers, of course, since that was his business per se. A few relatives he knew which still lived in the area. He was sure the rest would arrive by tomorrow, but most were unbeknownst to him.

Jack pondered the thought of his entrance to pay his respects. He knew it would cause a commotion, probably resentment by some, but as with the rest of his life he felt whether they liked it or not it was the code he lived by. His code of loyalty and honor, nobody was going to change that. He wasn't sure he should go in but he knew he had to.

Dressed in a conservative black suit Jack Rogin entered the subdued light of the funeral home. Without a hair out of place he solemnly arrived at the room that held his father's casket. Standing in the hallway at an angle he could see the whole room. Groups of people standing around talking all kinds of bullshit oblivious to the fact a dead body was at the front of the room when it was the only reason they were there.

Jack creaked his neck twisting it in a circular motion before walking in to the front of the room. As he stood there staring and thinking of his father he sensed the room grow silent as all eyes turned to him.

When he turned away he could hear the murmurs.

"What the hell is he doing here?"

"He's got a lotta nerve…"

"More brawn than brains…"

All the clichés he expected.

Jack stepped to the side and began to read who the flowers were sent by. An absentminded gesture to cover the feelings he was unaccustomed to feeling. The din of the room began to build when someone approached him.

"Good to see ya, Jack." Ted Coleman stood two feet in front of Jack's line of view. He waited till Jack focused on his presence, only because he knew Jack's mind was not on what he was looking at.

"Ted?" Jack was taken aback by the sight of his old friend. They had gone off to college together. When Jack decided not to pursue the life everyone had intended for him Jack's father had sorta unofficially adopted Ted as the prodigal son. Brought him into the firm as a junior partner which Ted turned around into a full partner. Ted knew his stuff and never felt he had his job handed to him. "It's good to see you, too. Honestly, I had forgotten all about you workin' for the firm."

"From the stories I hear I'm surprised you remember anything. Not that I believe any of it." He was quick to add.

"It's been a while. I don't remember all of it."

"Who does?"

The two men stood silently looking alternately between the coffin and the flowers.

"Listen, Jack, I heard a rumor you were at the hospital when your father died."

"Yeah? So?"

"Can you prove it?" Ted questioned.

"Maybe. Why?"

"It could be the difference between half a zillion and zilch!"

Tyler Martin remained quiet through dinner. I could see a lot was going on in his mind and didn't push for conversation. He would tell me when he was ready. The one thing he did talk about was renting a boat to do some preliminary dives at Crow Shoal to see what we were dealing with.

"See if you can get something that wouldn't attract too much attention, okay." Then almost as an after thought I added. "We don't wanna draw any fishing boats into the area either."

"We? I thought you couldn't dive."

"I can snorkel. Most of the area's shallow enough for that. Besides, this involves all of us, doesn't it? I'll be there."

"Okay. I'll make the arrangements, old boy."

"I'll be at the boat when you're ready. I wanna start the repairs on "Nightwind"."

"Whatever you need just ask."

"I should have everything already, but thanks just the same. Is Jack coming back tonight?"

"He wasn't sure, but most likely. Why?" Tyler answered raising an eyebrow.

"I'm gonna need some help probably. And I'd like to talk to him more about what happen in Rio."

"You think he's holding something back, too."

"No, it's just I heard this story years ago when it happened. All he really talked about then was the girl."

"With the way things are going she'll probably turn up too." Tyler mused.

We both smiled at the joke then went back to the silence that had prevailed before.

―――――――

"You mean to tell me, Doris never contacted you that your father was dying!"

"Not a word."

Jack and Ted had stepped outside into the humid air of the summer's night. Not a leaf turned in the stillness of the night air.

"You said you were sailing up the coast though, from Key West at the time, right?"

"Right. But we were never off shore for more then two and a half maybe three days. I'd always check for messages when we were in port. It's just a habit. Hell, I've been doin' it long enough."

Ted looked up at the stars and shook his head. Doris was Jack's stepmother. They had never got along from the first day they met. Doris had pushed her way into Jack senior's life after the death of Jack's mother. Five months later they were married. Jack knew without any proof that she created the biggest riff between him and his father.

Jack watched Ted watch the stars. Ted was a smaller man which made him look younger then he was. The sharp features of his nose and chin tended to distract you from the soft appearance of the rest of his face. His hair had recently been cut short and Jack couldn't help but ask, "Did they give you a lollipop with that haircut? I guess the pony was crooked, huh?"

"Damn, Jack, in twenty years you haven't changed a bit." Ted was more amazed then upset at Jack's carefree attitude.

"Lighten up, Ted. It's just the way I am. I can't change it. It's just the way I am. I'll find the humor in anything, especially when things are eating at me."

The night was hot because of the humidity and the air was still. They stood silent for a while before Ted started talking.

"Awhile ago, I guess when your father realized he was dying, he changed his will. At this point, I'm sure Doris knew nothing about it. Everything was set to go to Doris and her son. What's his name?"

"The fag?" Jack was sorry he said it as soon as the words came out. He really had no bad feelings towards Jim, just his stepmother.

"Yeah." Ted replied without reaction.

"Jim." Jack quickly replied.

"Yeah, Jim. Well anyway, your father changed the will in the event that you responded to his impending death. He left you as sole heir if you were there being you were his only living flesh and blood."

"You're shittin' me, right."

"Jack, there's a minimum of fifteen to twenty million dollars a year that will come into his estate. And that's not counting what assets he already has."

"I guess I was in the right place at the right time." Jack pondered.

"I'll say."

30

Binding Transitions

"I con't believe ju told dem all dat."

"I really didn't have much choice woman. The boat's fucked. I figured I'd be better off joinin' them since they're gonna be lookin' anyway. And they know where to look." Peter Winthorpe extinguished his cigarette in the ashtray next to the bed. He rarely smoked only when he was nervous or sometimes after sex. When he was really nervous he smoked a lot and sex was out of the question.

Peter lit up another cigarette watching Esmerelda pace back and forth in front of the bed. Her dark skin was visible under the sheer black negligé only now her mind was on other matters too.

"Ju said dey never told ju where it was. How can ju trust dem?"

"I got no other choice. He said he'd see to it that my boat would be fixed." Peter was silent as he blew smoke rings into the air. "Look, I don't much care for the situation, in fact I don't much care for him. I don't know, he just rubs me the wrong way, but I will say, so far he's been true to his word and over generous with his money."

"Dat be great. And how much does he want for all his kindness?"

"He never said and for some reason I really don't think it's important to him. It seems to be more like some sort of quest, or sumtin'. Like lookin' for the holy grail or some shit. For all of them."

Winthorpe sat back and smoked away as Esmerelda paced at a slower rate.

"What did ju say his name be again?"

"Tyler Martin. Why?"

"I be right back." Esmerelda threw on a robe and bolted out of the room. Peter knew she was headed into the guest room area but couldn't imagine why. He put out the cigarette he was holding yet forgot about as his mind kinda went blank with fatigue. He had just about passed out when Esmerelda raced back into the room.

"Petar, look at dis!" Emerelda shoved an old copy of Fortune magazine in front of him with an old picture of Tyler Martin. The article was titled "The Truant CEO"."

Peter's eyes opened wide as he began to read about how one of the richest men in America ran a numerous amount of business concerns from a pay phone. He didn't light one cigarette even after he put the magazine down.

"Ju tink maybe ju trust him now." Esmerelda coyishly asked as she pressed her now naked body against his.

"Yeah…it seems I may have miss judged the good man." Peter replied pulling her closer to him. They lay there silently enjoying the warmth of each other's bodies in the quiet room. "You better get some sleep woman. Breakfast time comes pretty early 'round here."

"Dat's no excuse, old man. I got me some help."

"What chu mean?" Peter questioned pulling back to see her better. "I can't afford you."

"Don't worry. Che won't cost ju nothin'. I put her in da old shed out back. For dat and some food I become a CEO."

She smiled at Peter and they both laughed pulling each other closer as other passions began to stir.

Amanda spent most of her evening in a whirlwind of cleaning activities. Not that the little shed was particularly dirty, fact was sometimes she couldn't tell what she had cleaned and what she hadn't. The point was it was hers. Not that she owned it or anything, but it was her place. Somewhere to come back to night after night. Someplace that would hold the things she wanted to own. Something she hadn't had in awhile. A home.

The excitement grew as she moved things around and placed them where she wanted them. She was home. She was in America. She knew she had money in an account somewhere. She would contact her parent's lawyer. She just couldn't remember his name, their names actually, but it would come to her, it had to.

Exhausted she decided to call it a night. Looking at herself in the mirror she was shocked at the woman looking back at her. She had almost forgotten cutting her hair off but the blackness of the dye startled her. Closely examining herself she felt the dark coloring made her look much older and she didn't like that. This would have to change as soon as possible.

Taking all her clothes off, she stared again into the mirror then shook her head heading toward the bed. A book she had found while cleaning sat perched on the table that she had squeezed between the wall and the already turned down covers. Lying naked on the bed she fell asleep before reaching the end of the first page. The book was all that covered her.

At thirteen minutes past two in the morning Esmerelda sat up in her bed next to Peter. The slight sound of the recoil from the explosion wasn't what had awakened her. The surge of evil in the cosmic blanket of the night had. It shocked her senses. She could see it in her eyes, blank yet staring. She could see it in the darkness.

Things the police would never see. The vevers smeared in blood on the dead woman's body and the car's interior. Signs of an evil that dwells in the darkest abyss of the Voodoo subconscious. All burnt away in the inferno.

Trying not to disturb Peter, she rose from the bed and began to pace the floor. She knew the meaning. Even without seeing she knew they had arrived. The men that had almost cost them their lives in Mexico. There was no point in warning Peter now. She knew in his own way he would be aware of the danger. Morning would be fine, let the poor man sleep.

Esmerelda stood at the window looking at the little shack out back. The light was still burning as her concentration focused on the ground where the light was cast. She looked at Peter and decided to go see how Amanda was. Peter would sleep but she knew Amanda was in trouble. Again she threw on her robe and headed down the darkened hall she had walked a thousand times before.

"Oh, My God!" Esmerelda rushed into the room after having knocked at the door without a reply. She had looked through the window and saw the frail white girl tossing about on the bed. The book had fallen to the floor and the only thing that covered her now was the sweat that drenched the bed she lay in.

Esmerelda quickly pulled the blanket over Amanda tucking the edges under her body. She went to the sink to soak a cold rag to use as a compress to bring Amanda's body temperature down.

Amanda tossed and turned mumbling words Esmerelda couldn't understand, but she understood what she was seeing. This woman was possessed by an evil that haunted the inner sanctums of her mind. Forces so deep in her conscious that her mind would never accept it as reality in her real world.

"Ju poor child. Sumhow I knew it be fate when we met, but sumhow I tink we gonna save each other." Esmerelda applied the cold wet cloth to Amanda's forehead with the immediate reaction of shock then a calm soothing relaxation of muscles that allowed her body to lie still.

"I shoulda knowed when I first saw ya, yer trouble girl. Guess I knowed you were cumin' though, jest wouldn't admit it."

Esmerelda pressed a cold glass of water to Amanda's lip's which she involuntarily drank. Amanda started to settle into a peaceful rest while Esmerelda shook her head.

"And dis is only da beginnin'."

When Esmerelda was sure the fever broke she left Amanda on her own. Amanda hadn't reached consciousness once during the three hour period.

Esmerelda returned to her own bedside where Peter still slept undisturbed. Laying in the dark with her eyes wide open she pondered the course that had been set.

31

The Road Back

*J*ack Rogin parked the Ferrari at the end of the wharf. The streetlights of Sag Harbor burned bright at his back as he stood beside the car looking out across the dark waters to Shelter Island.

"Fate's hand seems to be twiddling its fingers on this deal." Jack thought out loud. The discovery of his impending wealth left Jack's mind spinning. He had gone back to the office with Ted Coleman to discuss the situation and catch up on old times. After only a brief dialogue on what needed to be done about the estate Jack switched the subject back and forth between the old days, and his sailing adventure from the Keys. Ted caught on quickly that Jack didn't want to talk about the real issue and let it slide, for now.

They planned to meet again in the morning. Jack told Ted he had other commitments so he wouldn't be able to stay too long.

"It shouldn't take much, Jack. We just need to get a deposition from the nurse. Once you point her out, I can take care of the rest."

Now Jack watched solemnly as glimmers of the moonlight caught the ripples that broke the otherwise still surface. Ripples that created the exchange of swirling images between the two, light and dark. His thoughts wandered. Light and dark. All flowing together,

143

all flowing apart. His mind went blank as he watched the fluidity of the movement. All connected yet separate, each different yet oddly the same.

"Yeah, but what the hell does it all mean?" Jack mumbled aloud as a cloud blotted the moon from the sky temporarily before passing. He picked up a stone and tossed it far out into the reflected moonbeam which in turn created its own imagery. Turning to walk away to return to the car was when it hit him.

"Shit! Everything's connected, ain't it? One doesn't exist without the other." The moon had influenced all the subtleties he had seen. The flow of the tide, the refracted light from its glow, the darkness which was still unknown. His nerves were frazzled already, which was something he wasn't used to. His mind focused on his conclusion, but still this sudden realization hit Jack hard.

"It's because we're together. We're the stone. That's why it's all happening." We need to be together, to see it through to the end, Jack's mind imprinted.

Just as Jack was about to return to the car, a close yet distance explosion ripped the tranquility of silence that hung in the air. Jack jerked his head quickly to see the luminous flash of light from the blast before the echoed sound of the concussion bounced back and forth between the shores.

Suppressing his natural urge to check out the sideshow, as he often referred to accidents, fires and other catastrophes, Jack pointed the car to North Haven Peninsula and the south ferry, reasoning there were more important matters at hand.

"Hell, who ever would have thought I'd have more serious things to tend too?" Jack mumbled aloud as the wind jostled his hair while zipping along 114.

Tyler Martin had just gone below to bunk out for the night. "I'm too damn tired to row in, old boy. Besides, you're gonna be up early, right? Make sure you wake me." Was what he said before going down.

"Why?"

"Got a lot to do if you wanna get to the site before noon."

"Noon would be best if you want good light." Jack chimed in.

The events of the evening had taken a heavy toll on everyone.

The walk back from the Duval Cafe had seemed extremely long due to Tyler's pensive mood. Even in the pitch black of the only occasionally lit roadway I could see something was bothering Tyler.

There was no wind. The darkness that covered the island was total. In the distance from the road we could see a few scattered lights from houses nearby. The stars were brighter and more plentiful. There were no streetlights.

Silently, we had walked back to the "Nightwind". It had become a contest as to who would break the silence first. Tyler had barely said a word since the end of dinner and even then his thoughts occupied most of his time. I decided not to push it. I figured he would tell me when he was ready. It was weird. In some ways we were exactly alike, yet in others, as different as night and day.

I knew it was late. I had no idea as to an exact time. I hadn't worn a watch since I was seventeen. I was pretty sure it was after midnight, quite a ways after midnight. We hadn't seen a car pass since we left the main road back at the cafe.

Surrounded by darkness without a sound between us, we walked down the lonely road till my foot accidentally sent a stone skipping along the blacktop.

"Ha! You lose!" Tyler exclaimed sounding relieved for the intrusion of noise.

We both stopped in the middle of the road though we still couldn't see each other.

"Whadda ya mean? I wanted to do that."

"What are you talking about? You couldn't see anything was there. It's pitch black."

"I didn't hafta see it to know it was there."

Again the silence hung in the air. I knew Tyler was looking

right at me, I could feel it, but I was already trying to zero in on the last sound I heard from the bouncing stone.

"I'll bet you can't find it again, old boy." Tyler challenged as I knew he would.

"I'll take that bet." There was no mention of money. It wasn't important.

Gauging the distance with my steps I moved to the point of my best guess. In the stillness of the dark I stood there. I hadn't heard a sound from Tyler but I knew he was still right besides me. The darkness hid everything except the stars.

A swing of my foot just barely connected with something on the road sending it further down the path. The same sound bounced back that we had heard before.

"I guess it's your turn now, old boy." I whispered wanting to see how he would react.

Quick and quiet Tyler moved forward through the opaque night. He was good. Without the slightest sound in his movement he reached the last point we heard the stone make contact. Swiftly I countered his moves to remain at his side. When his hand reached out to touch me I blocked the move.

"So then my suspicions were correct, old boy." Tyler stated rather casually.

"Whatever do you mean?"

Tyler swung his foot bouncing the stone off the road.

"Haragei. Only one thing I don't understand, old boy. From what I learned of haragei, it's not just a receiving sense, it transmits as well. Yet, I don't pick up anything from you. It's more like an absence of presence, or something."

"I don't know what to tell you. It's been the same for me. I zero in on the lack of positive sensation. All I can figure is we're too much alike. Maybe we just cancel each other out, or something. I don't know."

"Interesting theory. Can't say I ever heard it before."

"Then again, maybe there's someone else out there draining

us that we don't know about yet." That sudden thought did not sit well with me.

"That's one I was trying not to think about."

We walked a while without a word till we reached the bottom of the hill.

"You know, I didn't want to push it but what the hell's eating you?"

"Skeletons." Tyler solemnly replied. "Let's find a place to sit a while. I'm getting tired."

Along the side of the road a large rock loomed up that seemed to fit our needs temporarily. So we sat adjusting our positions till the hard surface felt comfortable.

Tyler started talking almost right away.

"I'm really not quite sure what's eating me. More why actually. My mind has been rolling images of my past ever since you brought it up. The death of my parents keeps popping up for some reason, but I can't imagine what that might have to do with this."

Letting the silence smooth the edges I waited before saying, "That's something we never talked about. Maybe now's the time."

"Maybe." Again the quiet began to grow heavy before Tyler's words began to fill the night.

"My father was involved in quite a few smaller corporations, in one way or another. He was rich in the generally accepted sense of the word but mother was rich rich. From old money that just kept on growing. Apparently dad was always striving to amass his own fortune, shall we say to out do mom. Well, from what I've been able to put together, somewhere along the line he got involved with the wrong people. When he realized it, it was too late to get out. At least, on his terms."

"So what happen?"

The clouds had covered the stars and a light drizzle started to sprinkle us on and off.

"I still block most of it out. I only remember fragments of images. What I do vividly remember though is being thrown against a wall to watch my parents die. They didn't kill me though for some reason. I guess I wasn't important enough. I was only thirteen at the time."

"Maybe your destiny is to avenge their deaths."

"It's been a long time to keep believing that, old boy."

"Time has nothing to do with it. You should know that better then anyone."

"Maybe."

The rain had stopped but the clouds still blocked the sky. We started walking again.

"If yer don't mind my asking, do you have any idea who ordered the hit?"

"Yeah. I know exactly who. I could just never prove it." Tyler stopped watching the clouds move away from the stars before continuing on. "My father had kept a journal of his activities. It disappeared a few days after they died, but I know who he was dealing with. What I really want is the bastard who pulled the trigger. A short little prick with dead eyes. The punk was probably just a little older then me."

"Is that when you started martial arts?"

"No. That's when I got serious about it. What the hell was that?"

"Sounded like an explosion." We heard the reverberation bouncing around the atmosphere.

"Did you just get a chill up your spine, old boy?"

"Yeah." It was a feeling I didn't care for at all.

"Me too."

The moon and stars poked in and out of the clouds as we neared the turn for Ram Island Drive. In the stillness of the night we heard the unmistakable roar of a Ferrari. Moments later we were flagging down Jack.

"So, what did you boys do tonight?" Jack queried as we tried to maneuver two bodies into one seat.

"Not much. Just a quiet dinner."

"Hey, Jack, did you hear an explosion a little while back?" I had to ask knowing Jack's interest in sideshows.

"Yeah, but I thought I'd better head back. We got a lot to do tomorrow."

It didn't take any special awareness to sense the look Tyler and I gave each other. Our cramped little space on the passenger's side allowed little room for anything to go undetected. Luckily we reached the area where the boat was in about a minute and a half.

While stretching our legs after the short ride I was still thinking about what Tyler had said.

"You know, Tyler, you don't have to if you don't want to, but you never told me who put out the contract."

Tyler was bent over touching his toes before standing up to stretch for the stars.

"Some middle management asshole named Parker Webster, if it matters."

My head involuntarily jerked from the boat to my left. There on the hill barely lit by the late night sky stood the Inn.

"Oh shit!" was all I could mumble.

32

Dead History

"So where the hell is it?" Jim Macy was shaking Sheraton Quinn awake. Quinn had fallen asleep under the stars on the backbench of the Scarab. Macy had already given up trying to revive Bennington.

"What chu talkin' 'bout, mon?" Quinn replied dazed and increasingly annoyed.

"You know damn well what I'm talkin' about."

Quinn knew Macy's frenzied state meant business but he also didn't really care. Macy had no power over him, now or ever. When Sheraton heard the explosion, he hid the book in a crevice where it could have easily slipped at any time and no one was bound to look.

Macy mumbled something in disgust then went down below. A few seconds later he returned naked carrying his clothes. Quinn watched as he walked to the nearest trash bin and tossed them in, that was when he saw the blood on Macy's hands. Under the pile he held a can of lighter fluid and matches. After dousing the clothes thoroughly, the lit match did the rest. Again Macy came aboard, this time without saying a word walked to the bow and dove into the still frigid waters of Sag Harbor.

"Shit! What the fuck we doin' out here?" Bennington was feeling the pains of a hangover that had been waiting to happen for a long time. The "Quickchange" sat in the water outside Coecles Harbor waiting for something to stir.

Nobody on board was a happy camper. Bennington for the obvious reasons that grew worst with every small swell that lapped against the hull. Quinn because nothing was as he had dreamed it would be and his pockets were still empty. Macy for a lot of reasons. First, because someone beat him which still prayed heavily on his thoughts. Second, because his book was missing and so was Amanda, not that she mattered, but they were both points of his concentration. Pointers to the dark side. Third, was something he still hadn't been able to put his finger on. A face that looked familiar but still couldn't place.

He was slipping in his old age as his thoughts increasingly filled with dreams of early retirement. He was unaware the triad was complete. The time had come. The past was now one with the present.

Right now, the present was coming together for Casper Bennington as he made his way to heave ho the contents of his stomach into a choppy sea. The wind was blowing from the northeast over the open waters of Gardiners Bay. The "Quickchange" was presently pointed northwest. Casper chose the side to weather receiving half the bile he deposited back in his face as the wind whipped the water.

Neither Macy nor Quinn witnessed this little travesty since they were too transfixed on the entrance to the harbor. Too transfixed in fact to notice just how close to the shore they had drifted in the short time since the sun had rose high enough to brighten even the shadows.

Casper plopped down on the rear bench wiping his face off with his sleeve.

"Why the hell don't we just go in? What's the point of sittin' here? We can't see nothin'." Bennington wasn't happy.

"Yeah, and they can't see us either. What do you want to do, get close enough to check our teeth?" Even though they were within distance, Macy watched the harbor entrance through binoculars.

Quinn sat back smoking the last of a reefer Macy had handed him earlier. Quinn had the feeling Macy thought if he kept the black man stoned he could control him. Quinn really didn't care what Macy thought, he just wanted his money. And he hadn't forgotten any 'agreements' he had made with "Mistar" Bennington, but that was a supposedly larger piece of pie he was willing to let go for cash in his pocket.

"Maybe ju should tink 'bout movin', mon."

"Just keep your eyes open. They'll to be comin' soon."

Macy and Quinn watched as more boat traffic began to traverse the harbor channel. Mostly pleasure craft, a few sport fishing boats mixed in with a variety of sailboats and motorcraft. A Seatow entering the channel brought no special interest to either Macy or Quinn till they saw it return with "Dreamtime" in tow.

Macy fired up the engines to go take a closer look to see if any of his prey were aboard. Bennington let out a groan as his limp body spun from one end of the bench to the other at the back of the Scarab as Macy whipped the nose of the boat in the direction of the Seatow. The only sound louder than the grinding of metal against the shallow rocky bottom was Macy's yelling of obscenities at a crystal blue sky.

No one noticed the thirty foot Scarab Sport with twin two fifty Evinrudes shoving it over the water. Bennington was again retching his guts as Macy and Quinn surveyed the damage to the port engine. The prop needed to be replaced but the sheer pin gave before any serious damage had occurred. By the time they pulled their heads above the transom the Scarab was long gone. After a few minutes at full throttle it had cut its speed and was drifting closer to its destination with four men aboard looking into the depths of its waters.

––––––––––

Earlier that morning Jack had borrowed the car, and while Tyler said it was okay he appeared nervous. Jack said he would be back by nine thirty and though it was only twenty five after, Tyler had little hope for Jack's timely return.

We were waiting for the Seatow to arrive to take Winthorpe's boat to a dry dock for repair. Tyler had made all the arrangements by a little cellular phone I never knew he carried. Apparently, he was in more contact with his interests then I had imagined. Even the new boat had arrived during the night without any previous fanfare.

Right now my main concern was my boat. During the night we moved the "Nightwind", at my insistent, to a less conspicuous location in case anyone was interested enough to look. Apparently the damage to the boat's rigging was even less serious than I had originally thought. Now, with the help of Peter Winthorpe I was high on the mast refitting a new line when Jack phoned Tyler.

"Sorry, Dude. The season's on. Traffic's a hell of a lot worst then I had expected. I'm gonna be another fifteen twenty minutes, at least. Don't leave without me!" The roar of the engine barely allowed his voice to be audible.

"Don't worry, old boy. We'll be here." Tyler ended the call before telling us the news.

At the same time, Jack Rogin pulled the Daytona to the front center spot under the direction of the ferry attendant. He handed the guy a twenty for the one-way fare then walked to the rail with no interest for the change. Jack Rogin was going to be rich and it bothered him. His father's estate guaranteed a minimum of at least ten million for the next ten years. It could go either way depending on who was handling his interests after that period.

Ted Coleman's assessment of the situation was a cold look at the reality the way Jack saw it. In a lot of ways, it wasn't what Jack wanted to hear. Jack felt he was losing his independence. Sure, he had survived off the money without the need for employment but it was a survival. A limited budget, a no excess type of existence. Anything extra he got was out of the friendships he had acquired along the way, and with that, for some reason his mind kept returning to the girl he met in South America. How he wished with his newfound wealth he could help her in some way. Those were the thoughts that filled his mind as the boat gently nudged the not so distant shore. It wasn't long before Jack was boarding the new Sport with a fresh cooler of beer.

Tyler gently pulled the nose of the Scarab back off the beach. The power tilt lowered the engine till the boat planed smoothly across the rippled water to the new hiding place of "Nightwind".

"What's the matter, old boy?" Tyler yelled over the roar of the engines as the wind ripped the words into the distance.

"I'm not sure, I just hope we can put an end to the nightmare."

Jack offered Tyler a beer which he declined. Tyler also noted Jack didn't take one for himself either. He just stared at some distant point Tyler was certain only Jack could see.

In a few moments Winthorpe and I were on board and we were racing out the harbor entrance right behind the Seatow. It went one direction and we headed to where X marked the spot.

Jack's mind had drifted back to Rio. Remembering the time high above the city when he and the girl were tossing and turning with each other in the hot passions of eternal lust. All possibilities were being explored in a search for new heights of pleasure. Jack watched the crescent arc of lights that lined the boulevard trying to hold back as long as he could but she kept talking dirty to him and he liked it. And when it was all over they lay in each other arms satisfied. No fake moans, no fake orgasms, just pure sex. Hot and horny.

"You know, Jack, I never met anyone like you before." She knew she sounded stupid as soon as the words hit the air. "It's just...something..."

Jack knew she was a hooker but he said it anyway.

"I think I love you and I don't even know your name."

"It's Amanda. Amanda Paige."

Silently they pulled each other tighter as the moonlight and nothing else covered them in the Brazilian night.

The engines cutting speed brought Jack back to today as the Sport inched its way through Gardiners Bay.

"Good spot. Keep the marker to port. There's a rock over there somewhere." I instructed Tyler who was at the helm showing him with a pointed finger at the chart.

"Okay, old boy." Tyler replied with his eyes checking the depth gauge till he was sure we were dead center on the shoal.

Jack stood ready to toss the anchor. "That rock might be a good place to start."

Peter Winthorpe sat quietly watching in a pensive mood. The anchor was set and the boat drifted on the current to the outer edge of Crow Shoal.

"Let's get going!" Jack exuberantly shouted as he started pulling the diving gear from the storage chest.

"Ya think this is gonna be easy, don't chu. Well, that sand has been drifting around for over a century now." The anger in Winthorpe's voice was obvious, the reason wasn't. Of all the areas he had thoroughly checked none were as close to home as this one. He could see it from his tower. In fact he was looking at his tower above the tree line when Tyler began talking.

"We're not going to know what we're dealing with till we have a look, are we?" Tyler's tone was that of a man focused on his present task which was checking out his dive equipment. "You coming down?"

"I'll stay with the boat this round and keep an eye on things. I get the feeling we're sitting in the middle of a fish bowl out here." Winthorpe replied sounding somewhat despondent.

"Great. Then I can take a quick look around." I grabbed my mask and snorkel and was in the water pulling on my fins before Jack and Tyler were in their wet suits.

The water felt cold against my naked skin. Since I wasn't planning on being in long I didn't bother with a wet suit. The sun was high and the air was warm, so my body quickly adjusted as I made my way to the large rock that sat just a few feet below the surface.

Winthorpe was right when he said this wasn't going to be easy. We all knew it. All there was were a few pieces of waterlogged wood scattered here and there. Nothing to indicate that a ship ever went down here. Nothing that resembled a hull or any debris a ship might have carried.

I began circling around till I reached the outer edge of the shoal. It was Jack and Tyler's job to search the depths that surrounded it. They both entered the water as I was making my way back to the boat.

"Didn't see much." I said spitting the snorkel from my mouth.

"We'll poke around a little, old boy. See what we'll need for tomorrow."

"Yeah. Maybe we'll get lucky." Jack said putting in his mouthpiece before diving straight for the bottom.

I climbed back into the boat and threw my mask and flippers back into the holding bin.

"Yer friends got a lot to learn about wreck diving." Winthorpe's mood had altered little since I had gone in the water.

"Don't worry about Jack. He's been diving on wrecks since he was fifteen. He's just all worked up."

"What about the other one?"

"You mean Tyler?"

"Yeah. What's his story?"

"I don't know about his diving experience, but I do know he's a man who tends to find what he's looking for."

The only break in the silence the next five minutes was from the gulls and the water lapping at the boat.

"And what's your story?" Peter finally added.

"Whadda ya mean?"

"Well, you're not like them two." He motioned with his thumb at the air bubbles breaking the surface. "Fact is, I wouldn't be here now except there's sometum about you that scares me."

"Why's that?" I asked a little surprised.

"You've killed men before. I can see it in yer eyes." Winthorpe stated bluntly.

It wasn't a threat or a challenge, just a statement. I cautiously eyed Winthorpe not knowing what to expect next.

"I imagine the same can be said for you."

Winthorpe didn't let my remark sit for long before responding.

"Maybe, mate, but not calculated. I did what I had to do to survive."

"We're all just trying to survive, aren't we?"

Peter sat quietly staring out at nothing in particular before saying. "Well, I guess it's good we're all on the same side then. It should increase our chances."

It was the first time I detected the hint of a smile on Peter since he came aboard that morning.

"Ya know, Pete, I get the feeling there's something else we should know about."

33

The Whole Truth

*L*ate in the morning after all the guests were out for the day Esmerelda and Amanda began the daily routine of cleaning up the dishes and making the beds. The season was in full swing and the little bed and breakfast was booked so there was plenty to do. Amanda opted to start the dishes as Esmerelda headed to the rooms to make the beds.

"I'd feel more comfortable working in the kitchen for now, if you don't mind."

"I don't mind." Esmerelda smiled. "I hates washin' dishes." Esmerelda had yet to talk to Amanda about the night before. She wasn't sure how she should approach the topic.

What was this poor little white girl to think if I told her, "I think you're possessed by a voodoo demon, child.", Esmerelda thought to herself.

"She tink I be crazy." She said aloud shaking her head as she walked on down the hall.

Amanda's mind wandered as her hand swiftly washed plate after plate and the silverware. She kept drifting across little pieces of her dream. She was trying to put it together to make sense of it all.

Slowly the images began to come together clearly. She stood at the sink frozen with the fright that had grabbed hold of her as her thoughts began to again possess her very soul. Her staring eyes were fixed on nothing yet she saw deep into the dark corners of her mind.

This was how Esmerelda found her when she returned. Her body trembling covered with a cold sweat. Esmerelda shook Amanda to break her trance. The third time she finally awoke looking at her water wrinkled hands.

"What happen?"

"I was hopin' ju could tell me!"

"I don't know. I seemed to have blanked out."

Esmerelda sat Amanda down at the table and began putting cold compresses to her forehead.

"Ju and I need to talk, girl."

Amanda sat quietly as Esmerelda told her the fears she had that the girl had been possessed by some deity of the voodoo world. Amanda neither argued with her nor appeared shocked by the news. In fact, she seemed calm if not somewhat despondent by the whole thing.

When Esmerelda was finished she couldn't tell what Amanda was thinking. She waited for a response, ready for anything. Anything but the shock when it came.

"That God damn fuckin' Macy!" Amanda screamed.

Esmerelda's mind started reeling. She didn't really hear the list of obscenities Amanda was attaching to the name of Jim Macy. The one name from her past that sent a cold shiver through her heart and soul. The name of a man that killed as easy as breathing. The name she knew was lurking on the horizon ready to enter her and Peter's lives again. The name of the only mortal that had ever frightened her.

Once the two women calmed each other down, Esmerelda listened to Amanda's whole story. From the time she had met Bennington and Macy in South America till her island hoping back to the States crossed their path again and she became Macy's "sex zombie".

"Apparently, he fucked with my mind as much as my body." Amanda said in disgust.

Esmerelda sat pondering all that Amanda had revealed. She hadn't yet told her of her own encounters with these two men, or the fact that Peter had a run in with them in South America. She would wait till he was there for that. Now her fear of Macy had grown. He had used little known techniques of voodoo on Amanda. Powerful techniques that few would know.

"Da sex was a tool to open your mind." The black queen finally began to inform her.

"It tis used to impress de images wit out ju knowing. Ju probably din't know what he was saying but yer mind did."

Both women sat with their hands in their laps quietly staring at their own unforeseen spaces.

"So, what do I do now?" Amanda timidly asked. "How do I get him out of my head?"

"Da question is, what did he put in yer head?"

"What do you mean?"

"Right now, we only know der is a problem. We need to know mo to fix it. Tell me about yer dream."

"I'm not sure what I remember is right."

"Just start talkin'. It will come back."

"I remember a man in a gruesome mask hovering over me. I can't see his face but I know it's Macy. He's holding me down, sorta, but not touching me. I can't move. I want to get away, but I can't. I see red everywhere now. It's blood." Amanda's mind is slowly being drawn into the trance of the dream again. Esmerelda lets her slide listening for the key to help free her. "I'm covered with it. It's covering me. I can't breathe, I'm drowning struggling to get up but I can't. Oh God! Oh God!"

Esmerelda violently shakes Amanda quickly snapping her from her dream state. Amanda sits sobbing as Esmerelda holds her trembling body close slowly rocking her.

"Don't chu worry, child. Everting gonna be okay."

Later that same afternoon we arrived at the bed and breakfast in Peter Winthorpe's tow. He insisted we return with him before he would fill in any of the missing pieces to the puzzle. I don't know maybe it was the security of familiar surrounding or the support of his wife, but he wanted us there. I had been more interested in finishing the repairs the "Nightwind" needed but Tyler urged me to accompany him since Jack needed to go over to Long Island. So needless to say we found ourselves walking again.

"For a guy with a Ferrari you've been puttin' a lot of miles on those Capezios lately."

"Jack was going to see his lawyer again. I guess he's still tying up the loose ends with his father dying and all. Besides, I like walking, old boy."

"He hasn't talked much about that, has he? I wonder why?"

"Not to me." Tyler replied shaking his head.

Winthorpe had been quiet since we had left the boat tied to the mooring, but now he spoke as if he was mocking us.

"His name's Rogin, ain't it?"

"Yeah. Why?" I asked taking the bait.

"I guess you boys don't read the papers much, do ya?"

Tyler and I looked at each other and shook our heads.

"Well, your boy there's about to come into a lot of money, that is if his story checks out. It's been in all the papers, especially the local ones. Ya know, the prodigal son, bad sheep returns home."

"Great! I hope Macy hasn't seen it." Tyler said turning towards me. "We don't need him…"

Winthorpe stopped dead in his tracks grabbing Tyler by the arm until he had completely swung him around.

"Macy!?! What do you know about Macy?" There was a fear in Winthorpe's eyes that we could never have imagined existed there.

"He's here." I replied in answer to the question.

"You've seen him?" Winthorpe appeared more agitated with each click of the clock.

"No. I've never seen him, but Jack and Tyler had a run in with him and his partner a couple of days ago."

"So, Bennington's here too. He must lead a charmed life to still be alive 'round that bastard."

"Bennington. Yeah, that's what Jack called him. He's a doctor or something, right."

Winthorpe just raised his eyebrows then Tyler proceeded to relate the story of the incident in the bar. He finished just as we were walking up the front walk to Peter's place. By now, Winthorpe seemed a little more subdued, especially after learning Tyler had dumped Macy on his ass.

"You really tossed him, huh?" Winthorpe asked again in disbelief.

"Yep, but if you don't mind my saying so, old boy, you have yet to tell us what this is all about."

"That's why we're here, ain't it?"

Winthorpe ushered us into the foyer still shaking his head before leading the way through the house to a large kitchen at the rear of the building. We could have found our way by the smell of fresh baked muffins that filled the air. Esmerelda was in the kitchen alone pulling a tray from the oven when we entered.

The introductions were brief then Peter told Esmerelda that Macy and Bennington were here.

"Jes, I know."

Peter looked surprised at the lack of her surprise.

"How do you know?" Peter questioned hoping Macy hadn't seen her.

"Someone told me. Petar, we hafta talk. Now."

"That's why they're here." Winthorpe said pointing a thumb in our direction. "They need to know the danger that's involved now that the bastards are here."

Esmerelda shook her head in agreement.

Peter started by telling us of his original encounter with Macy and Bennington in South America. We listened intently as he told us how after they learned what he was after they began pressuring him to give them his information if he wanted to stay alive. He was sure they would have killed him if they had gotten his books which he always kept hidden. He anonymously tipped off the Government Bureau of Antiquities to keep them busy while he got away. It wasn't until he was in Mexico that they caught up with him again. With a small band of local thugs they ambushed Esmerelda and him, luckily the authorities happened to be closing in on the desperados at the same time. When all hell broke loose Winthorpe killed two of them with his bare hands. The federales got three more. While Bennington and Macy were thrown into prison, Esmerelda and Peter headed north where they eventually ended up on Shelter Island.

"We've been two steps ahead of them since we heard they killed a guard and got away."

"Til' now, dat is." Esmerelda added.

I looked at Tyler with a raised eyebrow and a slight shake of my head.

"He said it wasn't going to be easy. You wanna fill in the blanks or should I?"

"Go right ahead, old boy. I'm at a loss for words."

"Jack first ran into them in Rio too." I figured there was no point beating around the bush.

Both Esmerelda and Peter's eyes widened as I told them how Macy set Jack up to take the fall when the Antiquities Bureau came calling.

"I'm not sure of all of the details. You'd hafta ask Jack 'bout it. I do know he was involved with a girl down there but that's about it."

Esmerelda rolled her eyes, a gesture that didn't go unnoticed by anyone in the room.

"Is there something else we should know?" I prompted.

"Dis girl, you know her name?"

It had been so long since Jack had originally told me the story I had forgotten and looked to Tyler for help.

"I believe her name was Amanda."

At that very moment a tall lanky woman with short blonde hair entered the kitchen through the rear door. Amanda Paige had washed out as much of the black dye as she could before recoloring her hair as close to her natural shade as she could.

The room went silent as we all watched her enter.

"Sorry, I didn't mean to disturb you." Amanda shyly spoke.

"I was jest tinking of chu, child." Esmerelda walked over and took Amanda by the hand leading her to a chair by the table. When they were seated she carefully examined Amanda's palm.

"We haf met before. Do you remember?"

As if a light had flashed in Amanda's mind the touch of the black woman's hands caressing her opened her senses and her thoughts to a time that seemed so long ago.

"Yes. Yes, I do. It was on St…somewhere in the Caribbean. I remember you now."

"So do I." Esmerelda smiled.

"This world's just getting too small." Amanda smiled back.

"That may be the understatement of the century." Peter quipped.

"What do you mean?" Amanda asked with the puzzled look of a child on her face.

Esmerelda began to fill in Amanda on all that had been said and taken place, to which Amanda could only occasionally reply, "Oh, my god!" followed by Esmerelda telling us all that had happened to Amanda.

Tyler was trying to reach Jack with his little cell phone with no luck.

"He must not be in the car, old boy." Tyler said pushing the antennae back in.

"You mean, we trekked all the way over here when you could've called a cab." Peter was a bit miffed.

"I told you I like walking." Tyler smiled. "So, have we tied up all the loose ends?"

"Not quite. There's one thing I hafta tell ya Tyler. Not that it has anything to do with this, I don't think. I just wasn't quite sure when to bring it up."

"Well, go head, old boy. Now's the time."

"Parker Webster is the new owner of the inn."

The expression on Tyler's face changed from one of jovial interest to a blank stare. It barely hid his building anger. I tried to help put it at bay by continuing to talk.

"I only found out you had any connection with him last night."

"Don't worry. It's okay, old boy." Tyler said raising his hand as he calmed himself down. "I've always kind of known where to find him if I ever wanted to. Nothing has changed, I still don't have any proof. It is kind of weird though that he's here. Especially with all the other coincidences."

"Which brings up a good point..." Peter started to say before Amanda broke in.

"Yeah! Why are you guys here?" She questioned directly at me.

"Whadda ya mean?" I wondered.

"Well, mate, the rest of us, even yer friend Jack, are all tied to this in someway, mostly through Macy, 'cept you."

"I've only crossed paths with Macy recently, old boy. All of your connections span years, even Jack. How do you figure I tie in?"

The questions appeared to be dividing us.

"Dat may not be true." Esmerelda spoke up. "Perhaps dere was a time you don't remember. Both of you."

"I've never even seen this guy. I don't suppose any one has a picture."

Amanda was shaking her head no when Peter jumped up.

"As a matter of fact I do, mate." Peter ran off through a doorway that led to the tower where he kept all the items related to his search.

Amanda was telling us of her escape with nothing but the clothes she wore when Peter returned.

"These shots are from years ago, back in Brazil before I realized their game. And here's a clipping from a Mexican paper when they escaped. It's not too good though." Peter handed them to Tyler who was instantly transfixed by the image.

"This man is Mason James." Tyler's tone was steady and serious even in his shocked state. "I could never forget those eyes. This is the man who killed my parents. The man who worked for Parker Webster."

Tyler began explaining how he didn't recognize the older, heavier man in the bar but I didn't hear a word as the name of Mason James echoed in my own memory.

Jim Macy, Mason James. The same person? The same CIA spook that sold out my unit in Loas. Now the deaths of Sanchez and Nolan fell into place. The bastard was in both places at the right time. He could have easily done it. Maybe Jimmy's death was a suicide, maybe he just cracked under the pressure knowing that each day could be his last. My mind was clouding with thoughts past, present and future when Tyler's voice broke through snapping me out of it.

"Hey, old boy. What's the matter?"

"You look like you've just seen a ghost, mate." I felt Peter's hand on my shoulder.

As briefly as I could I tried to explain my apparent state of shocking comprehension. Everyone listened in a new awestruck intensity after just having heard Tyler's amazing story of coincidence.

"So, mate, yer tellin' us, this Macy or whatever his real name is, was a mafia wiseguy who joined the CIA."

"Basically, yeah. A real fuckin' patriot, huh?" I replied.

"Why would anyone hire an asshole like that?" Amanda was compelled to ask. "Specially, if you can't trust him."

"Yer can't trust any of them. They're all the same. It's just, they don't like to get their hands dirty. He does." I responded to Amanda.

"He down right enjoys it, mate."

"So, how do we go about finding him, old boy?"

"We don't. He'll find us. He's probably already watching us."

"Our third party." Tyler added.

"No doubt. I'm sure he'll wait till we find what we're looking for before he moves in."

"Find what?" Amanda questioned.

"I better try to get in touch with Jack again, old boy. He should know. He could be in danger."

"Jack? You mean Jack Rogin, here?" Amanda seemed bewildered by the sudden comprehension that Jack Rogin was actually here. Not just a name that floated on the air with all the other words.

"Yes, I'm trying to reach him now." Tyler answered her while punching the numbers into the phone.

"Jes. We all need to be here. We must fight dis evil together." Tyler shot me a glance as we both took note to Esmerelda's sudden empowerment. To us she seemed possessed with a new strength. To Peter she was empowered with a new energy that he knew would grow stronger when Jack arrived. All the pieces to the puzzle were finally coming together. Come hell or high water it was nearing a close no matter what the outcome.

Esmerelda took Amanda and went off to prepare what needed to be done for the evening's ritual.

Tyler still hadn't reached Jack but as we waited Peter began to fill us in on Esmerelda's strange powers and how they had already affected us all.

34

More Trouble

The "Quickchange" paced itself behind the Seatow that pulled Peter Winthorpe's boat at a slow methodical rate of speed. The captain was being extra caution not to get the crippled craft moving too fast. He didn't want to loss control which was what was beginning to happen to Macy. The snail's pace was wearing his patience thin.

"At this rate we ain't ever gonna get there!" He griped.

"Why ju followin' him anyway, mon?" Quinn was quite at ease with the leisurely pace blowing smoke rings just to annoy Macy further.

"We wouldn't be if you had been watchin' like you were supposed to!"

"I would haf bin if ju didn't decide to rearrange the prop."

"Will you two knock it off! My head is killing me. You sound like a couple of old ladies." Bennington shouted to his own dismay. His own voice only increased the pulsing pain clear to his toes. On his forehead was a cold wet towel that was doing little to relieve his throbbing head as the sun continued to heat up the air and humidity on this bright summer day. "Would you mind telling me why we have to follow him?"

Macy looked at Bennington with a smirk. At this point in time he only saw "Doc" and Quinn as a couple of loose ends that he would be tying up real soon.

"Okay…I'll tell ya. We missed the bastards leaving the harbor. The boat needs to be repaired. And we got nothing else to do till we find them again!"

"Okay. At least if we get the boat repaired we'll be ready for tomorrow."

"Right." Macy grunted in disgust. Yeah, and if they get lucky and find it today we'll never see them again, he thought to himself.

For the next hour or so no one spoke. As they neared the marina where Winthorpe's "Dreamtime" had been taken to be dry docked and repaired, Macy ordered Quinn to be ready with the lines as they approached the dock.

"Whatever ju say, mon." The touch of sarcasm in Quinn's tone didn't go undetected by Macy but was quickly forgotten when a voice from the past resonated through the hot, humid air.

"Mason? Mason James? Is that really you, you old sonafabitch?"

Macy was dumb struck and almost fell off the boat turning around so quickly to see Parker Webster walking towards him with an outstretched hand. Numb and at a total loss of words Macy reached out onto the dock to except the handshake.

"How the hell are yer, yer sonafabitch? It's been…god, too many years to remember. It's good to see yer still alive."

Quinn stood on the dock now next to Webster with his big yellow grin right in Macy's face while Parker continued to talk.

"Yeah, I'm retired now. In the hotel bizness." Parker continued.

Bennington sat there mildly amused at this sudden turn of events.

Macy on the other hand didn't hear a word that was being said or see what was happening around him. His mind was replaying the events of his last meeting with Parker Webster. How Parker told him he couldn't trust him any longer. How he would have to be eliminated. Well, Parker's first attempt cost him two men. The second only one. After that Parker gave up trying and forgot about it, but Macy didn't forget. Macy never forgot. Macy always swore he would get even with those who had crossed him. Even without his death list he knew the names.

"I'm sorry, boys. We haven't met, have we? My name's Parker Webster. I used to be Mason's boss, years ago. Ain't that right, Mason?"

Macy nodded in agreement with a deadpan expression glued to his face.

"Well, since 'Mason' wouldn't do the honors, Casper Bennington here." "Doc" offered his hand before pointing to Quinn. "And that young fellow there is my assistant, Sheraton Quinn."

"Pleased to meet you boys. You oughta come up to the inn for a drink."

"I don't think we'll have time, Parker." A tensed Macy finally blurted out.

"I think we might be able to squeeze it in, Mason." Bennington let the name hang there just to push Macy's buttons a little further. He really didn't care one way or the other about the fat old man who was dressed like an explosion of bad taste. How anyone could wear brown dress shoes with black socks that came to the knee under white Bermuda shorts with a plaid shirt of contrasting colors was beyond him.

"I said we don't have time, Casper."

Bennington sat there with his hands folded over the top of his cane that he had rediscovered. He smiled and shrugged his shoulders.

"What ever you think's best, Mason."

"I'll be seeing yer." Macy hissed.

Now it was Parker Webster who stood there dumbfounded not knowing what to say before he walked away in a huff. He didn't like being blown off especially by a little punk like Mason James. And that was his big mistake. He still saw Mason James as the same little punk he had used as a trigger man so many years ago. He didn't remember the details of their parting. He didn't remember enough about this mad dog to avoid being bitten. It would be three weeks after the events that were about to unfold before the remains of his body would be found. Events that were about to begin with Jim Macy's plans for "Dreamtime".

After handing the yard crew a few extra bucks to ensure "Quickchange" would be their first priority, Macy disappeared carrying one of his black bags leaving Bennington and Quinn behind to mind the boat during its repairs. The additional money really made little difference to the men's schedule of events. They had to wait for a piece that was being specially milled for Winthorpe's "Dreamtime". His boat was so old that no one stocked what was needed. It was expected to be delivered late that afternoon, so "Dreamtime" was on hold anyway. The half an hour or so they needed to change the prop and check its balance on "Quickchange" would just help kill some of that time.

Killing time was what Macy was thinking too. In the secluded parking lot on the far side of the boat yard Macy caught up to Parker Webster sitting in his car warming the engine while the baseball game blared from the radio. Coming up to the car under the cover of a roaring crowd cheering a home run, Macy artfully slipped the garret around Parker's neck before yanking it tight. The only sound that filled the air was America's favorite pastime.

After stashing the still limp body in a seldom visited area of the yard amongst the rotting hulls of old wooden vessels that lay scattered in various stages of decay, Macy thought to himself, "So much for little pleasures. Time to go to work."

Macy began pulling electrical components, wires and "C4" explosive from his bag laying out each item for assembly. His expertise was hardly state of the art, something the FBI noted after examining the remains of Betty Halsey's car, but nevertheless it was still quite effective. When Macy felt he had packed together enough explosive to blow "Dreamtime" out of the water he added a little extra.

"Interest for all the time I've been waiting for this." He thought out loud.

Everything was ready. Just connect one wire when he planted it and it would be ready to detonate. A radio signal would set it off when Macy wanted it to blow so he could watch the festivities.

After hiding the bomb in the boat graveyard in a spot that he could easily get it when the time came, Macy returned to Parker's car which was still running. He got in, adjusted the seat and the mirror and drove off.

———————

"Ju know mon, I'm gettin' mighty tired of sittin' 'round doin' nuting."

"Well, it wouldn't be long now." Bennington said matter of factly shifting his position on the bench. The yard crew was busy lifting "Quickchange" from the water as Bennington and Quinn watched and waited.

"Dis is not what I'm talkin' 'bout. I want my money and I want to get out, maybe before Macy decides to kill us in our sleep, or sumting."

"Nay, he wouldn't do that. That would take all the fun out of it." Bennington smiled at Quinn wondering why the black man was suddenly in a hurry to leave. He knew Quinn wasn't afraid of Macy. He had seen that in his eyes many times now. "Anyway, he still needs me to sell the prize once we get it."

"Dat be good fo ju, mon, but dat don't help me. I want my money and I want it now." The anger in Quinn's voice startled Bennington a little but not enough to show in his expression.

"Look, if I gave you what I have now you might be able to eat for a few days and not too well at that. Trust me, you'd be better off waiting a few more days. By then we should have some real money to talk about."

"What 'bout dat money in da bag?"

"The money in the bag? Oh! That's not my money. That belongs to the B&M Holding Company."

"What are chu talkin' 'bout, mon?"

"The B&M Holding Company is a corporation based in the Bahamas. They're the registered owners of the "Enya" and this new boat," Bennington stated matter of factly while pointing to "Quickchange". "I started the company years ago with Macy. It sets up a long paper trail no one is interested enough to follow, especially when we only pull into a port for a day or two."

"And what's all dis got to do wif my money?"

"Well, the money in the bag belongs to the corporation. We use it for operating expenses. Macy would have to agree before I could give you any of it, besides we still need it for now. The boat's got to be paid for, we still gotta eat and whatever else might pop up. Look, once we get hold of Winthorpe's treasure we'll blow this taco stand and head south again. I have connections down island where we'll be able to sell it for what it's worth. Then we pick up the money that's sitting in the Bahamas' bank and go our separate ways rich men."

Quinn had never seen any but he knew he was being snowed. He knew what he was going to do even before he started talking. Right now though, the name he had seen in Macy's book was his main interest.

"Dat be Petar Winthorpe will be followin'?"

"Yeah. Didn't Macy tell you who he was?"

"No. I guess he din't tink it was important."

"So? Why is it important now?" Bennington was confused. If Macy didn't tell him, how did he know the name?

"Well, I tink dat may be da same mon dat run off wif my sister, Esmerelda."

Casper Bennington's mind raced at the revelation. Putting two and two together things were adding up fast. New light was shed on Macy's activities of late. Now "Doc" understood how Macy came about his new knowledge of Voodoo. He was almost certain Macy was unaware he was being taught by the brother of the woman he wanted to destroy.

"The jerk never could see beyond the hand in front of his face." Bennington thought to himself while observing Quinn with new interest. Now he knew why Quinn didn't fear Macy like other men did.

"Doc" Bennington knew a little about Voodoo. Not any incantations or anything like that, but he did know a little about the history of its orientations and its uses. He wasn't afraid of it though. You had to believe in it to be afraid. He didn't know it could and had still affected him.

Jim Macy a.k.a. Mason James drove the late Parker Webster's big old Cadillac around the island. He needed to get away from Bennington and Quinn for a while. They were beginning to get on his nerves. He still realized he needed them though, especially "Doc". Without "Doc's" expertise in antiquities he knew he wouldn't be able to sell the piece once they got it for what it was really worth. "Doc" knew the real value of these pieces of history they had acquired and what the market would pay. He had the connections they needed to get the price they wanted whether it was legally or on the black market which was much more lucrative.

Quinn's value was minimal to him. At best he could be thrown to the dogs to slow down the chase if "Doc" and him needed to slip away quickly. Macy almost smiled at the thought of letting the black man live, after all he had decided Quinn would have to die even before he ever had a chance to use his lessons on Amanda Paige.

Macy slowly pulled the car to the end of the road before cutting the engine to look out across West Neck Harbor. He had decided long ago he didn't miss America. Sure there was money here, but it was harder to get and it never lasted as long. He had always felt confined by all the rules and the people who enforced them. With that thought in his mind he was about to start the car to leave when one of those people pulled his squad car behind the caddy with the lights flashing.

Jack Rogin's old friend Sam didn't have the slightest clue to the danger he was about to face. Sam had spotted Webster's car earlier being driven by a person unknown to him. He was busy issuing a speeding ticket to a day tripping tourist at the time but made a mental note to check it out later. Sam knew on a small island like this their paths were bound to cross again sooner or later.

Sam Watson's personal interest in Parker Webster started with the rumors that surrounded him when he suddenly brought the inn under what everyone deemed to be unusual circumstances. Rumors of his ties with organized crime, enough rumors to fill a book. Sam had been keeping track of Parker's activities when he wasn't busy with his other police duties. He was hoping he could catch the old man slip up, even if it was only a traffic violation. So far with no luck, but his interest was aroused seeing a stranger driving the old man's Cadillac.

Now his luck was changing as he spotted the car across the harbor at the end of the road. With only one way out he knew he had him and hightailed it to the point.

Jim Macy watched closely in the rear view mirror as the officer approached the driver's door from behind the Caddy. Another car filled with tourists stopped at the end of the dirt road. Macy patted the pistol strapped to his ankle for reassurance in case he needed it as the officer came closer. A sailboat and two motor boats were rounding the point at the same time. Too many witnesses to just eliminate the problem, Macy thought looking around.

Sam rested his hand on his hip holster as he swaggered to the side of the old Cadillac.

"Would you mind stepping out of the car, please, and keep your hands where I can see'em." Sam added as an after thought.

"Sure." Macy replied knowing he wouldn't need a gun to take care of this yahoo. "What's the problem, officer."

Sam picked up the distaste the words put in the stranger's mouth as he spoke them. They put a shiver up his spine. His hand automatically tightened around the grip of his gun as Macy exited the car. The words that left his own mouth now sounded weak, he was almost studdering. "You're not the owner of that vehicle you're driving."

Macy looked at the old classic car then back to Sam and smiled which didn't make Sam feel any better.

"No, I'm not." Macy let the defiant words hang in the air just long enough to see the sweat start to build on the cop before adding, "I borrowed it from an old friend, Parker Webster. Ask'em when you see him."

"I will. Mind if I see your driver's license in the mean time?"

"Not at all, only I don't have it with me. I forgot my wallet back at the inn."

"I see. Have any idea where I might be able to find Mr. Webster now?"

"Well, the last time I saw him he was in a boat yard on the other side of the island. I don't know the name."

"Okay, mister…"

"Mr. James."

"Okay, Mr. James, you can go for now but I'll be stopping by to have a look at that license later."

"Anytime, officer. Anytime." Cause I ain't gonna be there, Macy thought to himself as he watched Sam get back into the patrol car and drive off.

During their short encounter a dozen or more people observed the two men play out the scene. Sam Watson never knew how close he had come to dying but he still drove away trembling.

35

***

Changing Winds

*J*ack Rogin was beginning to feel better about his impending wealth. After explaining his dilemma to Ted Coleman about his loss of independence, they had worked out a plan that would pay Jack on a weekly basis out of a trust fund. The weekly allotment would add up to a little bit more than he was currently getting in his monthly remittance checks. The same fund would also support his step mother Doris and her son Jim. They could continue to live on in the house on Gin Lane as long as they wanted. Jack wasn't interested in the house at all.

Doris Kramer Rogin decided not to fight Jack's claim to the inheritance, of course that was only after Ted Coleman explained it would cost her more money then she had access to now. There were enough reliable witnesses to place Jack in the right spot at the right time. She didn't have a chance. Jack's wish to let them live as they were accustomed to while his father was still alive made the action senseless. The rest of the details would still need to be worked out and since Jack was the owner of the trust it could be altered at any time.

Now his main concern was hooking up with the guys. He had been to the boats only to find them deserted. Again he tried the car phone but for some reason it didn't seem to be working. So Jack was driving the rural roadways looking for a pay phone. When he reached the main route that ran through the center of the island he found one almost immediately. He pulled the Ferrari to the side of the road opposite the Duval Cafe and got out.

"Damn! Ten Million a year and I ain't got a quarter to make a phone call."

Jack looked around to the cafe then decided he was hungry anyway and headed across the street. After a quick burger and a beer he headed back to the phone with enough change to call long distance.

"Where you been, old boy. We missed you." Tyler sounded relieved to be hearing from Jack. Peter Winthorpe's tales of Voodoo had unnerved Tyler Martin plenty.

Jack explained to him there was a problem with the car phone and where he was now.

"We're at the bed and breakfast on North Ferry Road. On the left if you're heading north."

"If it the place I'm thinking of, I'll be there in a couple of minutes."

"Do hurry, old boy. We have quite a surprise for you."

"I'm on my way."

Jack hung up the phone and hopped into the Ferrari. With the pedal to the floor he sped north on route 114. He never noticed the old classic Cadillac that was following him.

When Jack reached the bed and breakfast, he pulled the car into the driveway. Macy passed the entrance then pulled the car to the side of the road just in time to witness the three men who came from the house to greet Jack.

"Well…it looks like somebody's luck is changing." Macy sneered aloud.

Esmerelda readied herself for the night's rituals. She would need all of her powers to drive the evil force away before casting a spell for protection against the unforeseen dangers that lie ahead over all of them. She felt the power surging within her body as she purified her soul of her earthly sins. A power stronger then she had ever known before, exciting her and terrifying her. She knew it drew its strength by countering the evil that was near. She felt her whole life had been preparing for this moment.

When she was ready she went to check on Amanda. Esmerelda would need to prepare Amanda too. Amanda needed to know what was going to happen. They needed each other more then ever now if they were to get through this.

As Esmerelda approached the door of the cabin she could hear heavy sobbing coming from inside. She gently knocked at the door which was ajar then slowly pushed it open. Seated at the edge of the bed was Amanda holding her head in her hands crying.

"What's da mattar, child? Did sumting happen again?"

Startled, Amanda's head jolted up wiping the tears from her face.

"Oh, I didn't hear you come in. No. I'm alright. Sometimes I just shouldn't think too much, that's all." Amanda wiped at the tears a few more times before getting up. She headed to the mirror and started brushing at her hair. "Look at me. What a mess!"

"Ju look fine, dear."

"That's not what I'm talking about!" Amanda snapped quickly realizing her injustice to Esmerelda. "I'm sorry. It's just…when I think of what a mess I've made of my life."

Again, Amanda began to cry.

"Now, now child. Don't chu fret. Fo all da forces workin' 'gainst ju, I'd say ju turned out alright." Esmerelda smiled her broad toothed smile. "Sure, ju're honest and sincere, and a berry likeable person."

"You think so?"

"Jes, I do. Now let's get ju cleaned up before dat fella gets here." Esmerelda took the brush from Amanda and started brushing Amanda's hair. They both stood there watching in the mirror.

"Do you think he'll still want me?"

"I don't think ju have to worry 'bout dat, child."

"Yeah, but this is the real world now. Things are different."

"Dat maybe, but some powerful forces brought ju two here at the same time. Dere's got to be a reason for dat."

"With all that's going on, what do you suppose us getting together again has to do with it?"

"Now how am I suppose to know dat. I can not begin to 'xplain why tings are as dey are, all I know is we are all connected in one way or another. Da control we have over what will happen we will see."

"You really believe in all this mystical stuff, don't you?"

"And ju don't?" Esmerelda eyed the skinny white girl curiously after all she had been through.

"I do, in some ways, but after what Macy did to me…"

"Macy is an arsehole. He tinks he can control and use des power as he wants, but he doesn't see da power controls him. It uses him for what it wants. Dat is why we need to be ready."

Esmerelda began to explain to Amanda what would be happening to her during the ritual Esmerelda would perform. This time she would be mounted by the true deities of Voodoo. Deities that would use her body for their own pleasures, pleasures that could only be enjoyed in the spirit world.

Amanda appeared to be growing a little nervous at her lack of control in the situation, but she held complete trust in Esmerelda. As the women talked and prepared, Jack Rogin's anticipated arrival had already taken place, but Amanda had already been swept up by the only powers that could save her from the grip of the madman.

———————————

"Wait a minute, let me get this straight," Jack was having a hard time believing all the facts as we knew them, "you're telling me it's all the same guy."

"That's it, old boy. Seems the same bastard has played a critical role in all our developments."

"I know I got some promises to keep." I blurted as my anger erupted.

"I wouldn't be so quick to want that, mate. No matter what his name is, he's still dangerous."

"Since when did you become such an old lady, Winthorpe?" I knew as soon as I said it it was uncalled for.

"Hey listen, mate, I've seen this guy kill peons in Brazil just because he was pissed off, and not even at them. If you want to go knocking on heaven's door, don't tell me about it cause I ain't interested."

"Sorry, Pete, it's just it's been a long time, now it's so close it's making my blood boil."

"I can understand that, mate." Peter almost mumbled after a long thought.

"So tell me again, old boy, what your wife has planned?"

"I'm sure I don't tell it like I should, but basically it's a purification rite."

"And that's gonna protect us?" Jack needed to ask.

"No, it ain't, but yer soul needs to get rid of yer sins before you can take on new strength. Spiritually, that is."

"Well, you can count me out." I wasn't about to take up faith in some religious hocus pocus for any reason.

"What's the matter with you, old boy."

"Nothing. I'm just a great believer in self preservation, at my own means. Survival because I make it happen, not because some unforeseen force is controlling my destiny."

"Influences from unseen forces effect you all the time, mate. Just look what the weather can do to ya. Time makes yer older with every tick of the clock, but we don't see that."

"That maybe, mate, but I still fight both of them on my own terms and I ain't gonna be there."

"Think you lost a convert there, Pete, but I'm game. How about you, Tyler?" Jack decided to jump in before tempers started to flare, which was probably a good idea.

"I've seen a lot of strange things since this thing started. I'm not going to take any chances especially if something might help. Yeah, I'm in."

"You sure you don't wanna reconsider, mate?"

"Thanks, but no thanks. I'll take my chances just like always."

"Suit yerself, but I think you're making a mistake."

"Well somebody has to keep a sober eye on you guys." From the corner on my eye I caught the tail fin of an old Caddy pulling away from across the street. I suddenly got a strange sensation, as if someone had just left the group that had been standing there talking with us next to the Ferrari.

"Did you feel anything just then, Tyler?"

"As a matter of fact I did, old boy. What was it?"

"I'm not sure, but I think we were being watched."

"You think bastard was here? And you don't believe in unseen forces, huh?" Peter's nerves snapped at the thought as he swung around trying to look in all directions at once.

"Could have been, Pete. Look, I won't worry about it too much. I still don't think he'll make his move till we find what we're after. All the same though, maybe we should have someone keeping an eye out at all times, yer know, sentry duty."

"I agree, old boy."

"Not a bad idea, mate. Maybe we can avoid any surprises before they happen."

"Hey, that reminds me. I thought you guys had a surprise for me." Jack blurted out.

The wind outside had stared to blow out of the northeast. With each passing hour it grew stronger. Inside the room was filled with flickering candles that scented the air with a sweet aroma. The howling sounds the wind made as it pushed its way through the old house added to the already eerie, ominous scene that was taking place.

Esmerelda stood in front of her altar swaying while repeating words that had been spoken for centuries. Her arms rose and fell with her voice as the sounds resonated off the walls. Kneeling by her side was a blonde woman with her back towards the three men dressed in white.

Tyler and Jack watched in awe not understanding the words the black queen spoke. They might have been having second thoughts about the whole thing, but like deer staring into the headlights they stood frozen in their tracks.

Peter knew the words, not that he could translate but he knew their meaning. He too waited and watched as the intensity grew. He felt the presence of the deities even before they mounted the two women. At that moment the music grew louder as the women began to dance, swaying to the rhythm.

As they turned it was then that Jack saw her face. Shocked he looked to Tyler who was enthralled in the scene before them for assurance. Returning his gaze back to the tall blonde woman only a whisper escaped his lips.

"Amanda."

Outside the wind was gusting close to gale force, now driving a light rain at a pelting speed ahead of it. Right now my boat was on the lee shore so I wasn't going to worry about it unless the wind came about. I had decided to walk the perimeter of the grounds just on a nagging feeling that something wasn't right.

In the dark driving rain I couldn't see much but I didn't see anything unusual either. I was about to reenter the house at the front when I heard glass shatter from the rear. Running through the house was the quickest way to the rear so that's the path I took stopping in my tracks just before the rear door. There on the floor was a chicken with its head severed but still hanging on by a sliver of skin. The blood splattered on the rear door was being splashed by raindrops that lessen the crimson color as it dripped to the floor. Now I bolted through the door immediately aware I was being watched. My senses were like an open wound.

Silently I stood in the rain. I could feel the presence begin to move away. I tried to stay with it as it took me away from the house into the open woods of the back property. I was expecting an ambush but it never came. The time I stood there waiting I realized the idea had been to draw me away from the house. Cursing myself I raced back to find more dead chickens scattered about.

Quickly I made my way through the house to the room I knew Esmerelda was using for her ceremony. From the outside the door appeared undisturbed, but I couldn't take the chance he hadn't gone in so I burst through.

What my eyes witnessed is hard to describe. The sense of being totally detached from their group was very much evident. As the darken room was flooded with the blinding light of the hallway, some took notice but I don't think anyone saw me, even those who looked. They all continued to dance and sway to the rhythm, even Jack and Tyler seemed to have fallen under the spell. My eyes surveyed the room to see if anyone lurked in the shadows. Not seeing anyone out of the ordinary I was about to leave when a glimmer of reflected light caught my eye.

In her dance Amanda Paige had swept a sacrificial knife from the altar as she passed moving in the direction to where Jack and Tyler were. In their present state neither were aware that she was approaching them.

Moving in I blocked her path which only momentarily confused her. With her eyes still closed she slashed out at me. I barely avoided the knife's edge as it passed close enough to slice my shirt. On her third attempt I caught her arm but her strength overwhelmed me, knocking me back with her force. Using a low roundhouse back kick from the floor I took the legs out from under her sending her tumbling to the floor.

When she fell Esmerelda's eyes jolted open. She had sensed the evil only as it had exited the room. When Amanda hit the floor the possession left her, only it was so sudden nothing else returned. Now she really was a zombie.

"Bring her here, quickly!" Esmerelda screamed out. The others were still unaware, trance like in their present state as to what was taking place.

Esmerelda quickly cleared a space near the altar. When I put down the body she wrapped it up tightly. Taking a bottle from the shrine she placed it to Amanda's lips forcing her to drink. All the time she was muttering words I didn't understand. The liquid made Amanda gag, it was the first sign of life I had seen. Esmerelda got up and started shouting more words. It sounded French or Creole, I wasn't sure. The others started to gather round not sure of what was happening.

Esmerelda grabbed a small bottle of what I later learned was holy water and a cross from the altar. Swaying as she recited the words she kept splashing Amanda with the water waving the cross over her the whole time. As the water hit her she screamed. Her flesh seemed to burn from its touch as she twisted in torment. This went on for more then an hour. No one said a word except for Esmerelda.

"It tis over. She be okay, fo now."

Peter took Esmerelda by the hand as if he were there to support her if she needed it. She directed us to take Amanda back to her cabin where she could rest. Jack picked her up with his massive arms and carried her from the room, he didn't say a word. He would spend the night with her applying cold compresses to her to help keep the fever down.

Explaining to the others what had happen, both inside and out, Esmerelda told me that rival Voodoo priests used the dead chickens as a sign that they had drained our strength.

"It tis not a berry good way, dough. Tis good ju were not here."

"Till the right time anyway, old boy."

"So, what happen with 'er?" Peter was puzzled. "I never seen anything like that before."

"Dat was not Voodoo. Dat be sumting else."

"Wasn't Voodoo, huh? She had the strength of ten men." I countered.

"If she said it wasn't Voodoo, mate, it wasn't Voodoo."

"Take it easy, old boy."

"Jes, Petar, please. We must'n let anyting divide us. We can only be strong togetda." Esmerelda paused, when she began again she was shaking her head. "No, I have never seen anyting like dat."

The room was silent as we all stood there though the wind still howled outside. My mind was drifting back to a memory of long ago.

"I have. Some intelligent agencies used a method of brainwashing that could be triggered at a later date. Sorta like human time bombs always ready to go off."

"Seems like something our boy Macy might know." Tyler suggested.

"He's had enough time with her to have done anything." Peter added.

"Think she'll be alright?" I questioned having seen Jack's concern.

"I tink so, but I can not be sure. Dis is new to me."

"Guess we'll just have to wait and see then, old boy."

Esmerelda and Peter left. Esmerelda needed time to regain her strength. She knew this was far from over. Peter would help her however he could but he even he knew this was going to take more from the both of them then it ever had before.

Tyler and I remained behind. As I looked about the room Tyler silently followed. I already knew the thoughts on his mind. It wasn't long before he asked.

"So, how do you go about deprogramming someone, old boy?"

"I don't think we can. Whenever we found out about someone before they were activated, we shot'em."

"What about after?"

"We shot'em, or they self destructed."

"Oh...I don't think Jack's going to want to hear that." Tyler's tone was somber.

"Yeah, well, I didn't exactly like saying it. We're not in country here, the rules are different." I stood looking around hoping for a better idea. "Hell, she was practically dead after she hit the floor. Whatever had a hold of her was gone. Who knows, maybe it's gone for good."

"You really think so."

"Not at all. Just wishful thinkin'."

Tyler and I left the room filled with smoke from the doused candles and headed back to the cabin to check on Jack and Amanda. There were no signs of our earlier visitor in the yard. Peter had cleaned up the dead chickens so none of the guests might stumble upon them in the morning before he had turned in for the evening.

We found Amanda tossing and turning, mumbling to herself like anyone else caught up in a bad nightmare. Only she knew what horrors were being played out inside of her head.

Jack sat at the edge of her little bed wiping her forehead with the cool wet rags that were helping her fever subside.

"They seem to be helping," he informed us, "her fever's down. She's starting to relax a little. Jack's voice carried more worry than he cared to admit.

"She just needs some rest, old boy. She'll be alright."

"Is that what the Voodoo witch told ya?" That same voice expressed a deep anger now.

"Take it easy, Jack. What's going on with Amanda has little to do with any religion." I tried to reassure him.

"Yeah, and I should listen to you. You almost killed her."

"Jack, believe me, the last thing I wanted to do was hurt her. When I saw her coming at you and Tyler, I knew something was wrong. I tried to stop her but she threw me against the wall with one hand. Look at her, Jack. She hasn't got enough weight or muscle on her to be able to do that. I had to take her down. There was no other way."

"If it was me, old boy, I would have done the same thing." Tyler tried to ease the burden Jack had placed on me. I'm not sure whether it shifted but Jack seemed to except what was done was necessary.

"So, what are you tellin' me happen to her then?"

"I think she's been programmed, brainwashed. By a professional, Jack."

"Macy?"

"Seems likely, old boy."

"So, what are we suppose to do now?"

"I don't know what to tell yer, Jack. Usually after their mission, if they don't get killed, they commit suicide."

"I don't like those answers." Jack seemed to focus on thoughts only he knew.

Amanda tossed and moaned momentarily drawing our attention to her as Jack doused her brow with water.

"She may be alright, Jack, I really don't know. There are other influencing circumstances here. Usually these people are real losers with nothing much going for them. That's what makes them easy targets and helps them remain unnoticeable till their time comes. I don't think that's the case here. Amanda got too much to live for. There's no telling how that will effect things."

"You're damn right. She's got everything to live for. I'll see to that."

Tyler stopped me before I said another word. He could see Jack didn't want to hear anything else. We left him with Amanda and headed back to the house through the steady wind and rain.

Sam Watson was having trouble seeing through the streaks of the old windshield wipers on his patrol car. The storm remained consistent and was expected to continue for the next twenty four hours. Slowly he drove along the parked cars at the inn until he spotted the old Cadillac at the end of the line. All the guests had stayed in because of the weather making the parking area more crowded then usual for that time of the evening. Even though he didn't want to, Sam decided to brave the wind driven rain and go in to ask a few questions.

He didn't like what he heard. No one had seen Parker Webster all day. And no one had ever heard of Mr. Mason James.

36

Final Countdown

$\mathcal{M}$acy had left the Caddy at the inn before returning to the boat to find a bored Casper Bennington twiddling his thumbs. Bennington told Macy, Quinn was below sleeping. The incoming storm had already started to stir things up, but that didn't matter to Macy as he put the boat at full throttle when they entered the choppy waters of Gardiners Bay.

The boat pounded its way through the wind whipped water until Macy was satisfied and decided to return to port at a more reasonable rate.

"Mind telling me what the hell that was all about?" "Doc" questioned once the noise level from the engines and the hull's pounding had dropped low enough to yell a conversation.

"Just testing the work." Macy replied tersely. "No tellin' what the weather's gonna be like when it's time to leave."

"Okay. Good point. I can accept that." Bennington begrudgingly agreed.

"Like you have the choice." Macy mumbled.

"What'd you say?" Bennington yelled back.

"What happen to your boy? I figured that would have shook

him up." Macy wasn't really in the mood for a confrontation with Bennington right now, though he considered it just a minor annoyance. He definitely didn't care where the hell Quinn was. His mind was on the men he saw talking outside the bed and breakfast.

Peter Winthorpe was a dead man, there was no question about that. He had been waiting a long time to write the conclusion of that little story. Now the only thing keeping him from finishing the job was the fact that his greedy desire was stronger then his basic instinct to kill.

Jack Rogin, he knew that face all too well, but Jack was only a minor character in the big picture to Macy. Jack's fate was marked the same, because according to Macy, he knew all the wrong people.

Tyler Martin, now there was a man he could really hate, even though his dead eyes had never seen him before that day in the bar. Only one other man had ever kicked his ass and lived, and that was a real long time ago. He never forgot about it either, as much as he tried. It still ate at him whenever he was reminded.

An unknown face with an unknown name for his little book of death. Someone he never forgot but didn't know or could ever really remember.

The fourth man, that was the man his mind kept coming back to. So familiar, yet unknown. He wasn't even sure he could remember what the guy looked like though he knew he would never forget him if he ever saw him again.

"He's gone!"

"Huh?" Macy's mind was far away when Bennington's verbal assertion barely registered on his psyche. "What are you talkin' about?"

"Quinn. He's gone." Bennington prepared himself for Macy's iniquitous reaction but it never came.

"Good. I was gettin' tired of his dejected puss anyway." Macy offhandedly remarked as he put the boat into a wide arcing turn.

Bennington decided to ride his wave of fortune and say no more, though he was personally pissed. He had trusted Quinn, and he had hoped to use him in his own plans of escape from Macy.

Darkness had already started to cover the sky when they finished tying the boat to the dock's side cleats that would help to protect it from the incoming storm. Macy looked toward the foreboding sky. Weather was something he didn't handle well. His mind wasn't quick enough. He couldn't adapt to the changes necessary to preform the tasks he had planned or were necessary at the time. Right now, all he wanted to do was find Quinn and kill him, but Quinn had to wait. The idea of disrupting his adversaries' activities was far more important to him right now. Anything to try to keep them off balance. Also, the odds against his eminent enemies had a greater chance of success then ever finding Quinn again, even he knew that. Quinn was one of the lost souls now much like Amanda Paige, destine to wander aimlessly until Macy again took control and ended their meaningless existences. So, with that praying heavily upon his thoughts, he began to plan his next action.

An hour or so later the wind driven rain was really getting on Macy's nerves. Pelting at his face made it even harder to see in the already dark shadows created by the trees. Cautiously he moved away from the bed and breakfast for the second time that evening. No one was following him now. He was sure of it. He wasn't going back. His run in with the stranger left him feeling like a raw nerve scraping sandpaper.

"Who the fuck is that guy anyway?" Macy mumbled aloud as he made his way through the woods back to the stolen car he used for his trip across to the island. He still sensed an unknown familiarity with that face which he hadn't been able to place. Every second it was making him even edgier.

"Ain't nobody that good. Nobody. Who the fuck is he?" The thought stuck in his brain as he started to drive with no particular destination in mind.

Wandering the back roads of the island, Macy's reflections drifted back to a time long ago when to relieve the paranoia that was beginning to obsess his mind he then joined the armed forces. After Parker Webster's two attempts on his life Macy was constantly looking over his shoulder waiting for the next one to happen. His nerves were becoming frazzled. Worst of all, he couldn't do what he liked best, because working for anyone else would have tipped Webster off to his whereabouts.

Quick history lesson, it was a time when the war was in full swing. Top story on the news every night put it right in front of you between the war itself and the protests against it. The draft was grabbing baby boomers children and ads to join up bombarded you everywhere.

The opportunity was perfect for Mason James, as he still called himself at the time. He could get away to a place where Webster would never think to look for him, or even try. Best of all, he could do what he liked best with no questions asked.

Only trouble was, questions were asked.

After a village on the edge of nowhere was found riddled with U.S. shells and the women raped, strangled or just cut up into puzzle pieces, lots of questions were asked but never really answered. Through a mountain high series of paper work, forgeries and corrupt officials Mason James was able to slip through the cracks until he became part of an ultra covert operation that was suppose to be undermining Hanoi's support from outside countries. What was most distressing about the arrangement though was it was so detached from any government ties it became nothing more then a loosely banded ring of organized criminal mercenaries.

Of course, Mason James fit right in. Before long he headed his own platoon of government assisted killers. The one thought that brought all this to his mind now though was one particular training session.

Two special groups had been brought together for a sort of clandestine war games; exercises in escape and capture maneuvers to be more precise. Tempers and egos were at the limits of cooperative behavior between the two rival factions. Macy's uncanny ability to elude capture without a trace to his whereabouts boosted his units points and his own already excessive behavior. He began taunting the opposition with verbal abuse raising anger levels beyond control. Shoving matches erupted fueled by the animosity that he was creating. The control of the commanding officers was being held by little more than a thread.

Then the officer in charge of the special forces group opposing the band of cutthroats ultra intelligence had organized sent in a new recruit to face the instigator. This particular recruit was so detached from the bravado antics of the other soldiers he had gone completely unnoticed by all except his commander, Captain Jack Morgan. Assigned to the captain because of some trouble he got into that involved the local authorities, this soldier's abilities were an officer's dream. He could shoot the wings off a fly at twice the distance of any of the services' best shots. Though it was his hand to hand combat skills that were even more impressive. Some of his instructors were even afraid of him. His defensive moves were pure survival instinct, fast and clean, but his offensive moves could be deadly. He didn't want to be there but didn't care either. He wasn't going to die until he was ready. So, when Captain Jack picked him to go against Mason it didn't make any different to him one way or the other. After all, it was just a 'game'.

They called it "the maze", though it was really a series of twists and turns that supposedly could be used for evasion or ambush maneuvers. The officers sat high above the pit, able to watch the progress of the exercises below.

The men entered at separate intervals through different openings, the lights went out and the time was recorded all at once. With infrared night vision equipment the officers were able to watch as the new recruit closed the distance to reach Macy in seconds. The touch that signified the hit obviously startled Mason as he was totally unaware of the other man's presence.

The lights flashed on.

"What the hell!?!" Mason's anger exploded. He looked into the face of the recruit never seeing it as the blood boiled in his eyes. Pulling a switchblade from his pocket he lunged for the seemingly unsuspecting recruit. The next thing he knew he was on his back with the soldier's foot pressing his cheek to the floor and his arm locked in a twist hold as the knife dropped sticking in the floor next to his face.

"It can't be! He's dead!" Macy's mind jumped back into the present. "I read the damn report."

Macy started to sweat. Fidgeting in the driver's seat he tried desperately to remember the faces. The faces he didn't want to match, but his mind drew a blank of both of them. The man that time so long ago and the other man at the bed and breakfast. That scared him even more.

"It can't be the same guy!" he yelled aloud. "It just can't!"

The words didn't convince him. Worry was something else Macy didn't handle well. A cold sweat began to trickle down his body sending a shiver down his spine. He needed to clear his mind. He needed to gain control.

He needed to kill.

He needed to re-empower himself through the blood of another. Just like he always had in the past, to draw his strength from the dead. Only now an uncertainty hung over him as it never had in the past. Now a real threat prevailed. A man with the abilities of this stranger held a real possibility of interfering with his plans. That was something he had never before encountered.

"What I need is some insurance."

An idea was already taking form in his mind.

The night was passing quickly but not the storm. The wind drove the rain in rhythmic sheets against the walls and roof of the old bed and breakfast. After a short sleep Esmerelda had awoke and was unable to sleep anymore. The power that had control over Amanda Paige frightened her, not because it had been so potent in its strength but because she had been totally unaware of its presence.

In her room with its altar mantel she sat contemplating what she knew as candles and incense filled the air around her with their scented smoke. Nothing had ever before passed unseen in this world that she probably knew better than any other living person. 'Any other living person' the words echoed in her head. With her eyes closed her body slightly rocked back and forth as she thought of her mother. A smile crossed her face. Her mother knew the power, her mother was the power and everyone knew it. They had lived in a land where everyone believed. Even the other priests respected the strength of her mother's influence. Her rivals never dared to tempt her powers.

Esmerelda's mother had gained the knowledge of her mother as her mother had learned from her mother. Esmerelda's great grandmother was said to have lived to be somewhere around a hundred and fourteen years old. No one was really sure but she had lived long enough to have blessed Esmerelda at birth with a touch of her thumb on the child's forehead. Her words foretold of a time in the future when she would need to call all of the power of the generations to help her. This is what her mother had told her. She believed that time was now.

She opened her eyes to see the images of her past generations standing before her. She raised her arms and began the chants that echoed back to an Africa many ages ago. For a long time that only seemed like seconds she continued till she felt the surge of power race through her blood. With her eyes still shut she thanked her mother and her mothers before her.

Still under the influence of these powers she opened her eyes to see a tall thin man walking towards her through the shadows of the smoky haze.

"I felt ju call her. Den, I knew ju were here."

"What are ju doin' here?" Esmerelda was stunned.

"I come as a warnin'. Ju do not know what ju are dealin' wif." Quinn was exhausted and confused. Not knowing where he was heading had drained his energy but the force of power emanating from Esmerelda had helped him focus his own origins again.

"And what would chu know?"

"I know more dan ju tink. Ju tink Macy is a disciple of Satin or sumting, don't ju? But ju are wrong."

"Ju know Macy?" Esmerelda's head spun at the shock of this sudden announcement.

"Jes, I do." The shame in Quinn's voice didn't go unnoticed. "He is not a disciple of Satin, big sistar. He is Satin. He is a dead man. Satin lives in his body."

"Dis can not be true!"

"Tis true and ju know it." Quinn stated looking away.

"So why have ju come here now?" Esmerelda questioned.

"I come because the power of our family has brought me to protect ju. Only, I do not know if I can. Da evil dat he carries is berry strong. Even he does not control it."

"But he is learnin', isn't he?"

"Jes. He is."

Esmerelda closed her eyes and again began the soothing rhythm of her rocking.

"Jes, dat maybe true but now we know it and we are strong." She spoke slowly with confidence.

When she opened her eyes again. Sheraton Quinn was gone. Only the swirls of smoke lingered in a room where dreams filled the empty spaces.

———————

When Esmerelda awoke she was in this same room. A few candles were still flickering in the drafty old house. Peter must have come in during the night because now she was covered with a blanket. Outside the storm blew at full force drenching the world as we knew it. The winds whipped the sea at gale force. No boats had ventured from port on this day.

In her awakening state, Esmerelda wasn't sure what was real and what was illusion from her encounters the night before. In her semi conscious dreamlike state anything was possible, not that it really mattered though, because warnings came in many forms. And only fools ignored warnings.

____

Little had been said between Jack and Amanda since she awoke at her usual early morning hour. Jack had been unable to sleep. He had been up all night worrying and hoping she was going to be alright. Now he quietly watched as she prepared breakfast for the guests with a total disregard for his presence. A silent barrier had gone up between them that neither one tried to breach.

When Esmerelda came in she was immediately grabbed by the tension that filled the air. As the clock ticked each click of the seconds grew louder. Perhaps Macy's powers were even more effective than anyone knew she thought to herself as she crossed the space between them to the counter.

Esmerelda poured herself a cup of the coffee from the pot whose aroma was filling the entire downstairs.

"Dat storm be blowin' pretty good." She offered Jack a refill on the cup he held surrounded by his hands. A nod but no words were his quick reply as he extended the cup so Esmerelda could reach it.

Peter bounced in looking much too chipper for the day after.

"We're gonna need to get out there as soon as possible. No tellin' what a storm like this might uncover."

"Well, count me out. I ain't goin'." Jack stated in tones that left no doubt for question. "I'll take the first watch."

"Suit yer self, mate. All I know is I wanna look."

"What the fuck yer gonna stay around here for. Yer think we need a fuckin' babysitter." Amanda screamed loud enough that it probably woke any of the still sleeping guests.

"Yeah, we all think you need a fuckin' babysitter." Jack stated in relaxed tones although his mood was definitely pissed. "Somebody's gotta keep an eye on our 'vulnerable' areas."

"Yeah, we all felt…" Peter began.

"Well, I can fuckin' take care…"

"I tink maybe ju men should leave so I can get sum work done." Esmerelda's voice boomed as it cut into the evolving scene. With a tilt of her head towards the door she indicated to Peter to go and take Jack with him.

"Cum'mon Jack, I got sumthing I wanna show yer."

Reluctantly Jack left in Peter's tow as Amanda stood with her arms crossed at her boiling point ready to explode.

"I tink maybe ju should get to work, Amanda. Peoples be cumin' down soon, okay?"

Like wind blowing at smoke Amanda's anger dissipated. She returned to doing her normal morning tasks without question. Esmerelda took note of the immediate change in her disposition. For now it was fine, the work needed to be done, but it also meant the forces they had witnessed last night still held their grip on her.

———

Peter led the way up the winding stairway into the tower that extended high above the rest of the house. Rain splattered against all the windows depending on how hard the shifting wind blew from any one direction.

"Nice view." Jack said looking through the distorted rain soaked panes of glass.

"You're the first one to see it besides me. I don't let anyone up here. Yeah, Esmerelda's allowed but she don't come. She respects it as my place."

"So, why'd you let me up?"

"I'm not sure. I guess deep down I trust you. All of youse. It's something ya can't explain."

"You don't have to. I know what you mean."

Both men silently watched out the windows as the storm blew in all its glory.

"I'm glad we're not out there." Jack solemnly said.

"I've been in worst, mate."

"So have I, but I'm still glad we're not out there."

"I guess, but I got the feeling we should be. This is the type of storm the Corona went down in."

"So?"

"I don't know. I just got the feeling we should be out there." The storm seemed to be throwing its final rage at the area as the men looked through the panes of glass. The pelting rain smashed against the glass on the east side of the tower. Both men gazed out across the waters to Gardiners Island when the image began to appear. A barkentine came out of the misty haze of the storm.

"Do yer see it?"

"Yes."

They watched without another word between them. The same scene Jack had witnessed while hanging as ballast from the "Nightwind" he saw unfold before his eyes again. Only now it was further away. After he shook off the initial shock he noted the exact position as the boat lurked into its turn. They were definitely in the right place. Only now he noticed something he hadn't seen the first time.

Someone jumped from the back of the ship as the first section of mast came crashing to the deck.

"Did yer see that?" Peter blurted out.

"Yeah. I didn't see that the first time. What do you suppose it means?"

"How the hell should I know." Peter's voice dropped off towards the end of his statement. For some strange reason he thought the sailor jumping from the ship was the same one he had seen on two different occasions. Though now he felt there was no point in mentioning it.

"I think you're right though. Someone should be out there as soon as this damn storm let's up."

"Amen to that, mate."

The two men continued to watch as the storm raged without another word spoken between them.

37

Reckoning Day

Wind and rain swept over land and sea throughout the day and well into the night. After midnight the deluge suddenly stopped though the wind seemed to intensify before its own wan just prior to the brightening sky of morning's mysterious twilight. Cloud cover kept the new day's light blanketed in a gloomy aura, creating the appearance of an unshadowed dead landscape.

The day prior, during the storm, Tyler and I went to the marina to check on what progress had been made on Peter's "Dreamtime". It was just a way of killing time so the day wouldn't end up to be a total wash out. For a change we were in the Ferrari instead of walking. When we got there the work crew told us "Dreamtime" was ready to sail with the promise of a delivery as soon as the weather allowed. Everything was better than new and she was running fine.

According to the experts at the meteorologist's center, the storm was expected to be leaving the area sometime during the night which was a close enough guesstimate for any of us to expect an early morning delivery.

Shortly after we departed, the marina had another 'unannounced' visitor also concerned with "Dreamtime". Cloaked by the wind and the rain he completed the task he had started the day before. Observed now only by the seagulls that huddled for shelter in any lee area they could find. He departed quickly letting the rain wash away his tracks.

The rest of the day for us was spent anxiously awaiting the promised change in the forecast while enjoying the dry cozy warmth of the kitchen in the old house. After breakfast Amanda had stayed in her cabin without speaking to anyone else. Esmerelda felt it might be better if we just left her alone for awhile. Maybe she would work out her problems by herself. Esmerelda really wasn't sure what to do about Amanda. It was a dilemma she had never faced before. Her biggest fear was that Amanda might leave without warning. She had entered the picture unexpectedly, she could disappear just as quick. That would not be good for anyone involved. Amanda was a definite piece of this whole sorted puzzle. Esmerelda knew that better than anyone. We all had to stay together if we were going to be able to stand against the evil power in Jim Macy. By leaving Amanda alone Esmerelda had hoped her anger would subside and her seclusion would help arouse her senses. Esmerelda was sure the need for others was within her no matter how deep she tried to hide it.

So now it was just a question of waiting to see what would happen next.

This morning on the dying wind I left the bed and breakfast to check on the "Nightwind" and continue the repairs which I still hadn't had a chance as of yet to complete. I felt a strong need to go down to the boat though, even if the storm was still blowing. I had been away from her too long already, maybe the longest ever, except perhaps that winter I dry docked her to scrape the barnacles off her hull. And all things considered, without a job the idea of returning to Key West early had crossed my mind. So I needed those repairs to get done.

When I got to the cove I found "Nightwind" had weathered the storm beautifully, just like I knew she would. The direction of the wind had never changed its bearing the entire time of the storm. There on the lee shore where I had left her anchored she was well protected by the high trees that lined the beach. Two additional bowlines strung from those trees had also helped keep her into the wind.

The marina had delivered "Dreamtime" at the first guess of light on a less than sparkling day. Now she drifted lazily at anchor probably less than seventy yards from "Nightwind" as I worked on the riggings.

All I had to wait for now was Tyler and Pete to arrive. I was expecting to see them to round the point any minute in the Scarab. Jack, I knew would stay behind because he already said he would. Even if his original reason for staying had been to be with Amanda, I knew he wouldn't go back on his word now that she had an attitude problem. No one really understood where she was coming from. In my mind I think everyone secretly hoped it would just be one of those woman things that would pass like the weather.

When the gleam from the nose of the new Scarab in the early morning light passed around the point it immediately caught my eye as she rounded towards my boat. I began putting back the pieces of hardware I was cleaning so I would be ready when they got there. "Nightwind" was ready to sail when they arrived.

"Where the hell ya been? The day's half over." I shouted when I thought they were within a shouting distance to be heard.

"That's what I bin tellin' him." Peter answered in a stern voice that carried well across the water. "We should've bin here an hour ago."

"Sorry, old boy. I figured the sun won't be high enough to light the bottom up enough to see anything anyway yet."

I tied the Scarab off from the line Peter threw to me. I wasn't about to get involved in this cat fight, but I must admit I was beginning to wonder just how much of Macy's influence was suddenly starting to wedge itself between us.

"Mind if I borrow yer rig?" Pete asked pointing to my dinghy tied to the stern. "I wanna check out my boat."

"No, go right ahead." I looked at Tyler with the question in my eyes, I thought he was in a hurry.

Tyler began to tell me about some larger metal detection equipment that would be arriving tomorrow while Pete started rowing towards "Dreamtime". He was about halfway there when I looked up to check on his progress. Then I glanced at "Dreamtime" and saw him, it, I don't know what you want to call it. Though even at this distance the image was unmistakable. He had on a striped shirt, black pants and a very old style sailor's hat with a patch over his left eye. Peter was rowing with his back to the image. He hadn't seen it yet.

Smacking Tyler on the leg, I grabbed his shoulders and jerked his body around. The sailor was waving Peter away from the "Dreamtime" only he didn't see it. We began shouting 'come back, come back' almost instantaneously. He looked at us and saw us pointing to his boat and turned his head. Then he saw it too and immediately began to come about, but it was too late.

Macy detonated the blast sending billows of smoke in the shape of a tall slender mushroom cloud high into the fresh morning air. He had been watching from across the bay when he saw Peter begin to turn. He never saw the warning we saw though even with his binoculars that were powerful enough to tell whether or not Peter had shaved that morning.

The explosion instinctively sent Tyler and me ducking for cover, but before the first reverberation echoed from the shore I dove into the water immediately followed by Tyler. As the smoke dissipated we could see the dinghy had capsized. Pieces of debris were still falling all around us. From the water level we couldn't see Peter so we swam even harder.

The sudden roar of the Scarab engines closing in on us caused us both to stop and look up. At full power but not yet at full speed "Quickchange" smashed my helpless dinghy into splinters in its wide turn before making its charge at us. We both dove for the bottom as the thunder above churned the water with its three slicing propellers.

Both Tyler and I popped through the surface at the same time after the speeding boat passed. We were okay but we still had to reach Peter. Luckily, Macy wasn't coming back for a second try. "Quickchange" was at full throttle heading for Gardiners Bay. We reached Peter's submerged body before Macy exited the harbor.

Tyler grabbed a floatation device from the debris of "Dreamtime" as I pulled Winthorpe's head above the water. We slipped the ring under his arms and began towing his limp body back to the "Nightwind".

"Is he still alive?" I heard Tyler's voice shout above the splashing water around us.

Answering Tyler wouldn't have made a bit of difference besides the fact I honestly didn't know. Peter was unconscious and wasn't breathing that I could tell. All I knew was every second he remained that way wasn't good.

Reaching the boat, I pulled myself over the side first then grabbed Peter. With a burst of adrenaline and a helping shove from Tyler, I yanked him into the boat on the first try. Immediately I attempted to empty his lungs of whatever water he had ingested. His heartbeat was faint but it was still there.

Tyler climbed in and went right for the first aid kit. Peter had cuts and scrapes all over his body from the flying debris of the explosion, none of which appeared to be life threatening. The exposed areas of his flesh took the brunt of the damage though he did receive quite a serious blow to his left temple.

Tyler snapped open some smelling salts from the kit and stuck it under Peter's nose. At once his eyes popped open, he began coughing up water in a fit that only allowed for gasps of air.

"That sonafer bitch!" He managed to get out between coughs. "I'm gonna fuckin' kill 'em."

"Relax, old boy. You're in no shape to be killing anyone. You've had quite a bump on the old noggin. Maybe you better rest a while, stay ashore today…"

"Not a chance, mate. Can't yer see? We're close, real close. I just know it. He knows it too. That's why he's already tryin' to lessen the odds to his favor."

"He might have a point there, Tyler." I had to chime in. "I know I wasn't expecting him to move in before we had it."

"And maybe he's just wacked, old boy, and doesn't subscribe to your logic."

A bad feeling swept over me when Tyler spoke those words.

"Tyler, where's yer cell phone?"

"On the boat." He said with a directional thumb.

I jumped over to the Scarab.

"In the bag, old boy." He shouted as I looked around.

Surprising myself I remembered the number to the bed and breakfast on the first dial.

"Esmerelda? It's me. Is everything okay there?"

"No. Tit isn't. Amanda is gone. When I went to see why chi hadn't cum to help me aftar breakfast, all I found was da note."

"Is Jack there?"

There was a long pause of silence at the other end before she finally answered.

"No, he isn't."

"Did he go looking for her?" I had to ask though I was sure that wasn't the case.

"I don't tink so. Evin aftar he knew she was gone he stayed."

"So, what aren't you tellin me?"

"When I went to look fo him aftar I had didn't seen him fo a while I saw blood on da ground." She hesitated before adding, "It looked like sumting bin dragged away, I dunno."

"Get yerself into town and stay around people you can trust. Stay visible. We'll talk to yer later."

I hung up the phone to the staring eyes of Peter and Tyler. I cut right to the chase.

"Jack's missing. Macy's got him."

"What about Esme...?"

"She okay, but Amanda's missing too. Probably ran away."

Both men were solemn in their thoughts for what seemed like an eternal silence till Tyler started to speak.

"Well, old boy, if we're gonna get Jack back we better go find what Macy wants."

"Getting Jack back alive ain't gonna be that easy."

"I know," Tyler gravely answered, "but let's take one step at a time, old boy."

"Right, mate. Besides the only way to find the bastard now is to have him come to us."

"He's already come to us and we weren't ready. We've lost one man, hell almost two, and there's a woman somewhere out there that can cause us a lotta problems."

"Listen, mate, this is just the beginnin'. We're gonna see more trouble then you can ever imagine in the next twenty four hours. And it ain't gonna end when we find this thing either."

"We got no other options, old boy."

"Look, I ain't arguing with either one of yers. I'm just saying we got to get ahead of this bastard somehow, that's all."

After bandaging up Peter's abrasions we boarded the Scarab and headed out to the shoal. We all knew Macy was out there somewhere watching. We could feel it. Tyler was sure he spotted "Quickchange" but it was at such a distance he couldn't be sure.

The boat drifted forward as we inched up unto the shoal. Peter looking old and worn in his makeshift bandages was at the helm as I prepared to set the anchor. The wind had begun to shift and the clouds were darkening as we crossed the open water of the bay.

"Not like the weather man said it was gonna be, is it mate?" Peter said with his eye on the clouds as I tossed the anchor.

Tyler was under the surface before the boat was taut on the line. With him he carried a small submersible metal detector he picked up at the dive shop. Even before he reached the bottom he began to scan the area in a sweeping motion. Using imaginary grid lines in the sand he covered every inch of bottom surface and plant life starting with the rock as his central fix.

The bay was getting rough again as the wind began to whip the water making snorkeling practically impossible but I gave it a try anyway. With the clouds growing continually darker visibility under the surface was being reduced to an arm's length at best.

So, after my failed short attempt to have a look around I rejoined Peter in the boat.

Silently we watched as Tyler's air bubbles moved methodically along their path.

"He's watching us, mate. You know that, don't cha?"

"Yeah. I know it." I answered to get a fix on his location.

"No. I mean right now, this second. I can feel the hate in his eyes burning me."

"Well there's nothing we can do about it now. Even if we knew exactly where he was and we made a move, he'd be long gone before we'd ever get there. He has to come to us. We just have to be ready this time."

Again, the sounds of wind covered the silence between us as the bubbles broke the surface constantly moving further away.

"Look, mate, I wanna thank yer for savin' my life before." Peter suddenly blurted out almost embarrassed by the gesture.

"Don't mention it. I'm sure you would've done the same."

"Don't take it personal, but I'm not so sure anymore. I'm gettin' too old for this kinda crap. I been askin' myself a lot lately why I been puttin' my life on the line for so long. I got nothing to show for it."

"You have a wife and a successful business, maybe that's the real treasure of Shelter Island. That's more than a lot of other people have." After saying it, I thought he might have thought I was referring to myself but that wasn't at all what I meant when I said it.

"Yer right, I know, and without Esmerelda I would have nothin'. She's the one that's been holding it all together so I can go out and play pirate." He seemed to be pondering his words before adding. "I think I owe her a lot more than any treasure could ever give her. Whether we find the damn thing or not, I think the time has come to quit."

"That's your decision to make, Pete, but all the same at this point in the game it seems to me you'd still have that nut job, Macy after you for your passed discretions."

"Does seem the tides of time have brought us all here for the final showdown or sumthin', don't it?"

Briefly we watched across the bay as the wind began to lash at the water with a sudden fury. The skies darken and day turned to night.

Tyler broke the surface probably because his visibility had gone down to zero only to be tossed around like a cork in a child's play pool.

Then we saw it. Tyler saw it too. Appearing within the darkness from nothing its shadowy specter intensified as the rain briskly swept over us. Three masts set with full sails stood high above us. We could see the faces of the men in the riggings working desperately to reef the large heavy sails. A barkentine so close we could read the name.

"Corona."

We heard the mumbled shouts of men trying to get her under control. We heard the muffled crack of wood against the rock below and the snap of the tall mast that sent her spars crashing to the deck within a tangle of lines, riggings and men. The ship let out one loud groan as she lurked sideways snagged by the bottom. She swung right through us and we could feel the energy of her time as she passed. Then she disappeared maybe for the last time.

I looked to the spot where Tyler had been only now he was gone too. I wasn't sure what to do. I grabbed my fins and mask. Peter seemed to be in some kind of dumbstruck awe, unmoving his hands were glued to the rail. I was about to enter the water when he yelled.

"Thar he is!"

Peter's excitement was bursting out of control, because there in Tyler's hand held high above his head was the object Peter had spent a lifetime in pursuit of, the golden dagger of Cortez.

"He's found it! The sonafabitch found it!"

"Damned if he didn't," was the only awestruck response I could muster.

Before Tyler even made it back to the boat his cellular phone began to ring incessantly. I flipped it open and waited to hear the voice on the other end. I knew what to expect.

"If you wanna see ya friend again I wouldn't get too attached to that little trinket." What it was I'm not exactly sure but hearing Macy's growl coming through the phone enabled me to precisely pinpoint where he was hiding. I turned to look directly at him as I spoke.

"I wanna know Jack's okay."

"Well…he's not exactly okay…but he is still alive, for now. You'll have to trust me on that. If you wanna keep him that way be on the wharf at three, and I mean you pal, not your friends. And don't be late, I don't like to be kept waiting." Macy cut the call. I pointed my finger at him in a gun like gesture. I knew he was still watching. A shiver ran up his spine as my thumb hammered down indicating the shot pointed right at him.

Angered he smashed the high power binoculars against the deck from where they proceeded to bounce in several pieces into the bay. Now even more pissed he went below to punch the already bloody and battered face of Jack Rogin. The fact that he was tied and strapped to a chair was the only way Jack's semi conscious body managed to stay erect.

"Is that your best shot, Ace?" Jack was barely able to mumble.

Macy hit him again.

"You better lay off him, Macy, if you want to keep him alive long enough for bait." Bennington had let more than enough pass. He knew Macy was out of control. Macy had seen his golden idol, his grail. Bennington knew nothing would stop him now.

This situation wasn't going to fit in with "Doc" Bennington's plans. Casper Bennington liked America. He liked the cosmopolitan way of life, nothing at all like the third world cesspools he had been passing time in of late. Passing time was the key. Any crimes he had ever committed in this country were way beyond the statue of limitations. Now he wanted to stay.

The wharf was crowded with the usual amount of summer tourists, probably even a few extra for a weekday. The weather had cleared and it was the beginning of a long holiday weekend. The sky was crystal blue with only a few puffy white clouds floating lazily by casting their unnoticed shadows on the earth. Aromas from fish, food and boat fuel wafted gently on the shifting breezes over the wharf. The revelers noise mixing with the sounds of gulls and motor engines made each little group seem like a private party.

The bastard said three o'clock and I was here. If Macy had learned anything in the time that had passed since our last encounter it was that crowds distracted from the ability of someone gifted in haragei to pinpoint an adversity lurking at any distance. Then again maybe it was just the stupid luck his kind seem to always carry with them.

Moving through the dense crowd it was hard to see beyond the next group, there were so many people, not to mention the cars cruising back and forth looking for spaces to park where there were none.

As the intensity to the situation grew in my psyche the look on the faces around me showed their instinctive fear at work as they scurried away. My eyes scanned the area like radar working the grid, but even still, Macy or Jack could have been ten feet away but I didn't see either one of them anywhere. Then I decided I was going about this all wrong. Instead of trying to pick up on Macy, I should be trying to zero in on the pain I knew Jack would be suffering.

With my attentions switched I started to get an inkling when a voice cut through the air right besides me. Then I saw her.

"If looks could kill!" Amanda shouted.

"Amanda!? What the hell…you better get outta here now! Macy has Jack, and he's coming." Her expression quickly changed to the zombie like state I had seen her in the other night.

Slowly turning in the direction of her stare, I saw Macy approaching with Jack Rogin propped up next to him like a shield. Macy was smiling. Jack's face was swollen and bruised with signs of blood still trickling from his eyes, nose and mouth.

The sightseers began to distance themselves from this scene as Macy closed the space between us till he stopped ten feet in front of me.

"You okay, Jack?"

Macy's gaze concentrated on Amanda who remained motionless. "I had worse playing football." Jack mumbled with an attempt to smile. Macy twisted one of his broken fingers sending the agonizing pain throughout Jack's body till it registered on his face.

"Where is it?" Macy growled.

"It's here." I replied pointing to my left without looking. I knew Tyler would be there standing at the edge of the dock with the dagger. Peter was right below out of sight in the boat.

"Tell him to bring it over!"

"First let Jack go."

"No." Macy pulled the gun he had been pressing into Jack's back into the open pointing it directly at my head. "Tell him to bring it over now!"

Bennington had been watching everything unravel from the opposite end of the wharf. Standing on the dock he held the umbilical cord that was their lifeline to the only way out, "Quickchange".

"What the hell is he doing? He's out of his mind!" Casper blurted aloud to himself. Right then and there he decided to abort the mission and dropped the line into the water.

Immediately "Quickchange" started to drift away from the dock on the ebbing tide.

Ted Coleman had been fishing with his two sons at the end of the wharf oblivious to what was happening fifty yards behind them when he saw the line splash the water. He yelled to Bennington.

"Hey, mister, your boat slipped her line!"

"It's not my boat." Bennington replied then tipped his hat covering half his face before trying to mingle with the scurrying crowd. He still had to get past Macy and needed the opportunity to do so.

"Hold on cowboy." I said with one hand raised to Macy. I nodded to Tyler who started to slowly walk towards us.

Again, Macy had the advantage and there didn't seem to be a damn thing I could do about it. I misjudged him again. I didn't think he'd pull a gun in a public place. Not that it really bothered me that much but I didn't want to see bullets flying with a bunch of innocent bystanders around. I needed something to happen soon to change the course of things; to open that door of opportunity. It did.

"Freeze right there, asshole!" Sam Watson shouted from a little further back from where Amanda stood. Sam was off duty in street clothes but he still carried his service revolver. He had seen Macy pull Jack from the boat. He had been trying to get closer ever since.

Barely looking in the direction of the voice Macy fired two shots. One bullet grazed Sam's temple, the other caught him in the shoulder. He went down to the tarmac hard. His gun slid directly in front of Amanda. Sorry to say, Sam never learned you can't reason with a maniac holding a hostage. Shoot first, then read him his rights.

Macy started cursing at Amanda in words I don't know, a mix of french or latin, I'm not sure. Again, in her trance like state, she reached down to pick up the pistol. After dropping Jack to the pavement in a heap of flesh, Macy shouted more words I couldn't understand, then some I did.

"Kill'im. Just kill'im." Macy growled with one finger pointed to Jack while his gun still pointed directly at me.

Amanda held the gun in her right hand. Her body trembled as she tried to raise it. She took it in both hands and lifted it through the convulsions of her sobs. Jack lay motionless on the ground with his back to her.

"I said kill'im!" Macy shouted venomously at her again.

Amanda trembled then shook violently before her head turned away as she let the gun drop to the ground.

"No!!!" She screamed back like a banshee. The fire of her life had returned to her eyes. "No!!!"

"You stupid bitch!" Macy sneered pointing the gun at her as he squeezed the trigger at the exact instant Casper Bennington raced over to knock Amanda to the ground with a side block. "Doc" took a bullet in the leg for his valiant effort that was meant for her.

In the same breath that all this happened, a tall thin black man approached from the edges of the crowd raising a small black book above his head. The symbols on its cover was directed at Jim Macy. The eyes rolling back into his skull appeared to glow red as Quinn began to spout words rarely heard in the modern world at the center of this evil we were all facing. All at once Macy was doubled over clutching uselessly at his pain. I took the opportunity to move in and attack. A solid front kick to his head sent him sprawling to the pavement, it also broke the abstruse hold Quinn had over him.

As Sheraton Quinn continued his oration the book burst into flames in his hand. He threw it onto the pavement in a cloud of smoke and ash then disappeared gently into the mass of people that gather to watch this spectacle.

Macy was groggy but he was already up. Tyler was close enough to take the gun from his hand with a crescent kick, but Macy didn't care. He wanted me in a more primitive manner. He charged like a bull only I was expecting this type of attack. I took all of his energy into a back roll and tossed him over onto the pavement a good ten feet away. Again, he was up right away. Now we were face to face.

The sounds of sirens filled the air around us but the authorities still hadn't been able to penetrate the throng of people that were blocking the entrance to the wharf. The rage in Macy's eyes frighten all that were near enough to feel the evil in their intensity including Tyler who began to back step with the dagger still in hand. Peter had climbed to the dock when he heard the shots, rushing over to Jack as fast as his own throbbing pain would allow. Amanda was joined by Esmerelda who appeared from nowhere in the crowd of curious onlookers to help aid Casper Bennington and Sam Watson whose condition was a lot more critical. Quinn was gone, disappeared into the crowd as I stood face to face with this maniac alone as the crowds tried to abandon the area.

Macy came at me with a series of punches all of which I countered except the double right at the end which grazed my head. He threw a left front kick which I sidestepped to avoid with a right grab then a left inside block which off balanced him sending him to the ground again. I realized the mistake right away. I had the chance to break his leg and I didn't. This wasn't just survival. I had to maim or kill this bastard with every opportunity I got. I paid for the mistake.

At first the sting was just a minor annoyance. As Macy rolled from his fall was when it first hit. The pain increased rapidly. I looked to the pulsating spot on my thigh to see a small dagger protruding from my flesh. The second one whizzed past my ear as I instinctively ducked which saved me but helped increase the pain in my leg.

Sunlight caught the edge of the blade Macy was now wielding in my direction as I still lay on the ground. Backing off in a cradle stance I managed to kick out with my good leg catching the bastard solidly in the side of his knee. I felt the crunch of his joint more than I heard it snap as I scraped back along the pavement. The jolt only appeared to slow him down momentarily but it gave me enough time to scramble to my feet.

The pain in my own leg had gotten about as bad as I thought it could get, which was good because now I could control it, in a way. I knew what moves I could make and still be effective. I knew what I couldn't do too, and that was making me mad. I had made too many mistakes waiting to see what this bastard would do next, not anymore.

"C'mon cowboy!" I taunted him as the sirens came closer. "It's just you and me now. And time's runnin' out!"

Macy attacked slashing the large knife through empty air. With sweeping blocks I avoided the first two cuts catching his wrist firmly with the third swipe in his unbroken rhythm. A smashing blow with my free hand snapped his elbow from behind putting his arm into a position I'm almost certain it had never been before. The heavy knife dropped into the hot pavement with a thud burying the razorsharp steel point a good two inches into the hot blacktop, but Macy still managed to swing his injured arm back like a dead weight catching me with a glancing blow to the side of the head. I was beginning to think this guy could feel no pain.

That's when I realized.

Of course, this guy didn't feel any pain. He was supposed to be the embodiment of evil, after all, wasn't he? An apparent believer in the powers of voodoo and all its darker customs. He probably was all doped up too. He'd feel the pain alright but its effect on him wasn't going to be any time real soon.

Macy swung the broken arm at me again. This time I ducked coming up with a solid sidekick to his ribs. The sound of bones cracking made the gawkers in the surrounding crowd wince in disgust but it didn't even slow Macy down.

The sky began to return to the gloomy aura it held earlier in the day. That mystic sense in the air that had been with us every leg of this journey. Thunder rolled in the distance as erratic flashes of lightening began to brighten various portions of the sky, like the flickering intense light of an arc welder trying to repair the damage in the cosmic web of the universe. Tyler realized what was happening. He had become a real believer in the powers that control the destinies of the world we pretend to know.

Retaining a true essence of non being Tyler drifted closer like a wind blown smoke, changing but always present. Then without hesitation Tyler Martin slipped the pointed edge of the jeweled dagger between Jim Macy's ribs.

Macy dropped to his knees in a tormented wail of angered pain that would have killed the average man. It was as if the golden dagger had cut an ever growing black hole into the basic source of the evil that had sustained his very being. Lightening ceaselessly flashed violently in the surrounding skies as the ever blackening clouds thundered all around us. Macy's anguished screams even covered the pulsating sound from the authorities' sirens as they finally made their way into our little world of mayhem. Even gunshots couldn't stop a sideshow long in this town, especially during season, as was evident as the crowd had almost doubled by now.

Without precipitation or warning, Macy abruptly surprised all of the gathered menagerie by managing to jump to his feet as if unscathed, then sprinted to the edge of the wharf where he expected to find "Quickchange" ready and waiting. Dumbfounded he stared momentarily into the distance watching as she bounced on the wakes of the vessels trying to avoid her in their passage through the harbor. Then as quickly as if inspired by her name Macy ran to the opposite side of the wharf knocking Ted Coleman out of his way in the process. Ted was only trying to protect his preoccupied sons after witnessing this raving maniac when he found himself swimming for a ladder. Macy looked as if he had been propelled off the edge of the wharf freefalling precisely in time to stranglehold a jet skier from the watercraft he had been riding illegally within the harbor.

The last we saw of Jim Macy he was skipping across the water like a stone with the dagger bouncing in his back as the jet ski slapped against every wave in its path. The storm seemed to follow him though the skies remained dark.

Everyone the authorities questioned later would describe the scene as a war zone which made it apparently obvious they had never been in a war but the media loved the use of popular catch phrases.

Triage implemented with the paramedic's arrival wisely chose Sam Watson as the first candidate. The graze to his right temple left him with a headache and a burning sensation that wasn't going to stop without some aspirins and lotion. His real problem was the shoulder wound though. The bullet tore through the flesh but by some miracle it didn't shatter any bone. The problem was it didn't want to stop bleeding. They were busy tending to him now.

Jack Rogin was a sorry sight but given a little time to heal he would be okay too with a slew of new aches and pains to let him know the changes in the weather. Looking at him made me glad I never played football, if he really thought that was worse. I could tell though the real pain he felt now was in his heart. Lying on his back barely conscious of what had happened he watched from afar as Amanda was trying to comfort Casper Bennington.

"Why did you do it, "Doc"?" She questioned as the paramedics tended to his wound.

"I dunno. I guess you're just too…I dunno…full of life to let a bastard like Macy take that from the world. You make this world a nicer place to live in, Amanda." "Doc" squeezed her hand in what was probably the most tender gesture he had ever offered her.

Amanda turned her head as a tear rolled down her cheek. "I can only thank you, "Doc"…but I don't love you."

"I know that, Amanda. It's okay, I understand. Believe me, I saw it today. That was the one reason why you couldn't shoot your friend over there," Bennington pointed with a flick of his thumb, "Jack. Macy could never understand anything like that. A power as strong as real love could never be broken by even the darkest magic. Why do you think he could never beat that damn Brit and her," he said pointing again. "You better get over there now before he thinks we're havin' some kind of affair or something."

"Thanks again, "Doc". I'll never forget you."

"You better not." He replied with a sarcastic chuckle.

Amanda kissed Casper Bennington on the forehead then ran to Jack in tears.

Esmerelda held Peter's head in her lap stroking lightly at his brow. Winthorpe's wounds were minor by comparison to the others, besides the fact his had already been amateurishly attended to. Presently he was expressing his disappointment to the only man left untouched, Tyler Martin.

"But why the hell did yer hafta use that to stick him with. It had to be worth a couple of million at least!"

"Nope. Only eleven hundred and ninety two dollars and thirty five cents, to be exact, old boy."

"What the hell yer talkin' about. That was a god damn Aztec relic."

"Not that one. You didn't ever get a really good look at it, did you old boy?"

The puzzlement on Peter's face was obvious, it was also obvious now that Esmerelda's only concern was that Peter was okay. She didn't give a damn about anything else. She didn't even look up.

"Not really." Peter mumbled after thinking about it. "Only when yer first got outta the water and even then ya held it the whole time. We pretty much rushed right over here after that. You kept it under wraps the whole time."

"I had it made, Pete." Tyler said as if embarrassed. "Sorry, I didn't tell you but after the things I have seen in the last couple of days I couldn't take the chance of someone else knowing it was a fake. It wasn't the real thing, old boy. I had a feeling they might pull something like this. Bait us with no options. Something where we might need a little insurance."

"But how did yer know what it would look like?" Peter questioned even more perplexed.

"I didn't. But I figured no one else did either. That's why the biggest problem in this crazy new world I recently fell into was I couldn't even take the chance of telling someone else. From what I've seen letting anyone else have that knowledge bouncing around on their brain waves somewhere could have ruined everything."

Peter fumbled around in his upper shirt pocket to pulled out a still damp Xerox copy he had of the dagger. They could have used it as a model to forge the one Tyler had made.

"I made a copy of this from the book my ancestor left behind, mate." The sketch was crude but showed enough detail to define its unique form from other pieces. "You gonna tell me it didn't look like that."

Tyler held the paper in his somewhat trembling hands, staring in silent bewilderment before handing it back to Winthorpe.

"Let me see." I took the page from Winthorpe glancing it over as I spoke. "I only saw it briefly in the bag when I went to get the phone. I couldn't tell ya any differences," after perusing the sketch. "From what I saw though, I didn't think you'd be able to stick it in him."

"It was pretty crude, wasn't it, old boy?"

"Yeah, it was, but that's not exactly what I meant. I really didn't think you'd be able to muster yourself to do it. You're just not the killer type."

"To tell the truth I wasn't sure I'd be able to either, but as I got closer, in my mind's eye, I was overcome by the past. It broke me out of my nightmare more than anything else. It had to be done. You gonna get that tended too, old boy." Tyler suddenly changed the subject referring to the dagger still protruding from my throbbing leg.

"There's nothing I'd like to do better, but Jack and his cop friend there are in a lot worst shape than this. Besides, as long as I don't pull it out I don't think I'll bleed to death." I only half joked looking at the still slow trickle of blood on my thigh though my thoughts were concentrated on the boys in the suits that were moving in closer. "Tyler, the keys in the boat?"

"Don't tell me you're planning on leaving us, old boy?"

"Yeah, looks like the time has come."

"You know, this could be the time to…"

"Come in from the cold? Look, Tyler, I really don't know what you think, and now's not the time to discuss it. I'd just rather remain anonymous, okay. I've got no crimes to answer to. My worst transgressions would probably be the lies I tell to the women I meet. I'd just like to keep things the way they are, okay?"

"Okay, old boy." At first I thought he was just pissed off when he walked away but then I realized he was creating a diversion with the two approaching men in the grey suits.

Heading to the boat was my only desire only that would have been too obvious. I drifted towards "Doc" Bennington now being attended to.

"Thanks for helping Amanda." I bent down sending sharp pains through my leg as I picked up Casper's hat and cane. "I'll buy ya new ones."

"Thank you. I would probably have been dead by now if it wasn't for you. I've never seen anyone go against that bastard and live. Keep'em." He shouted referring to the pieces I took while I slowly walked into the crowd cane in hand with the hat dangling over the blade still protruding from my leg.

Escape was beginning to look impossible. Every inch of the wharf was covered by the police or government agents. They were tying up "Quickchange" at the point where "Doc" Bennington had let her line slip away. They were questioning a dripping wet Ted Coleman who sat under a blanket someone had provided next to his sons. Sam Watson was being loaded into an ambulance surrounded by the curious. Different arms of law enforcement had converged on everyone left. Now the safest route seemed to be the quickest route; straight to the unseen boat.

Slowly turning I started to hobble in that direction but suddenly I stopped with the crack of thunder that ripped through the now almost cloudless sky. Turning my head back I saw the swiftly changing skies hovering over Crow Shoal. As the light faded the darkening sky spread closer, the "Corona" sailed again.

I took the opportunity to race towards the Scarab.By the time I had the engines running a thick fog had blanketed the area. I crept away slowly rounding Shelter Island on the far side almost making a complete circle before reaching the "Nightwind".

Epilogue

That day on the wharf happened a long time ago. A few months after I slipped away, I started to hear bits and pieces of what transpired that afternoon in Sag Harbor.

Amanda Paige pleaded her case to all those connected that "Doc" Bennington shouldn't be held as an accomplice. Since no one could control Macy anyway, why should Casper be held responsible. If anything, he was the dupe, a victim as much as the rest of them. Tyler didn't care one way or the other about Bennington, and Jack only had a slight grudge which instantly dissipated at Amanda's reminder that "Doc" had saved her life.

The real problem to this line of thought was Peter Winthorpe. Peter had almost lost his life and Esmerelda's at the hands of Bennington and his maniac killing machine, there was no denying that.

After letting him brood awhile though, Esmerelda's calculated persuasion made him give it up.

"He'd be free now too, Petar. He save dat little girl. Macy be gone and so es da dagger. Led it go, mon. It be time to live again. Wif no shackles to hold us."

When the time came Peter told the authorities he couldn't remember a "damn thing". The explosion had scrambled his memories like pieces of a jigsaw puzzle in a box; they might all be there but he wasn't going to be sure till he put it all together again, and that may take some time.

Amanda basically told Jack the same thing only she remembered a little too much. She was afraid of trying to make a commitment to him and scared to death if she didn't. She felt almost as bad as she did when she woke up in that murderously hot room aboard the "Enya"; sick to her stomach, not sure why and unable to guess what her next move should be.

Jack really had no concerns about Casper Bennington at all. He could barely recall his hazy image from his drunken days in Rio, but he did feel cheated he would never get to face Macy, one on one, instead of being blackjacked from behind. His tortured body wanted revenge, his heart wanted it too. Macy was to blame for his untimely separation from Amanda in he first place. He knew his imagination couldn't begin to fathom all he had put Amanda through. Besides all that, he had been run out of towns before but never out of a country. That was something he wasn't going to forget to easily.

Sam Watson had a long recovery with a lot of time to think. He quit the police department a living hero. I heard he was selling life insurance or something like that with all the zest of a man who had been at the brink of death.

When the time came, Tyler Martin, called in all the cards. Without hesitation, he used his name, wealth and power to hold the authorities at bay like children waiting for ice cream, which was longer then I needed. When he saw the silhouette of "Nightwind's" sails as she left Coecles Harbor beating against a rare east wind, he demanded he speak to his lawyers before answering any questions. He insisted he was the victim not the perpetrator here and felt he was now being harassed by the so called local justice system not to mention the Feds. After being attacked by a lunatic they obviously had no control over he complained now that his civil rights were being violated.

Ted Coleman jumped at the chance to represent Tyler Martin which helped push his own name to national limelight through the media's growing interest. Ted actually turned out to be an excellent attorney with his quick wit and ability to adapt. Tyler took him on as his personal counsel and kept him long after this little circus blew over.

In another strange turn of events that evolved in the aftermath, it seemed that Ted Coleman was associated with the firm that represented Amanda Paige's parent's lawyers at the time of their death. From what he remembered off hand a sizable amount of money had been put away in an interest bearing trust fund just waiting for the return of their daughter whose whereabouts were unknown at the time.

My luck seemed to be holding too, in its own way. I think I had seven dollars in my pocket when I sailed away but I managed to catch a fish or find something stored away that I had forgotten about. I was never too hungry or too broke the entire time I headed south.

Even when I was in port at Charleston, South Carolina, an early hurricane hit us directly. I had decided to sail up river before hand and had found a safe little cove that was probably only big enough for three boats. Only one other kept me company at the time I was there and I heard close to three hundred had sank or were damaged back at the city.

I made it back to Key West unscathed only to find Lorraine had slipped further down the globe. Nobody was quite sure where anymore. I worked day sails on the boat and bartended for cash at night.

Jack and Amanda stormed into town after their first kid. Five weeks old and he was out to see the world. Jack's excuse was he was looking for me. He said with my sudden departure he never got a chance to say goodbye, and I think he meant it too cause after two days they headed back home. He told me both him and Amanda were in rehab. Together they had a new outlook on life and this town was just too tempting.

Jack also told me Tyler Martin had committed himself to the corporate world and his religion. Apparently, Tyler had been deeply involved in Judaism in his youth but when his parents were killed shortly after his bar mitzvah he had lost all faith. Something changed that after his encounter with Macy. Now it was time to grow up, apparently not being able to save his parents left him feeling less than a man. Tyler said he had regained true control of his self and his assets too. Money was being lost and people were being laid off, that wasn't the way Tyler Martin did business. Jack felt what Tyler was really trying to do was keep his mind occupied so as not to think too much about the new world he discovered. The one in which he couldn't help but believe in but still tried to deny.

I never heard from Tyler Martin again though occasionally bills were paid for without my knowledge.

If Casper "Doc" Bennington wasn't a crook before all this started he definitely was one now. Casper had opened an antique shop on Madison Avenue. The prices he quoted for any one piece were beyond the realm of honest trade but he always got the money, in cash. Turned out Casper Bennington held a P.H.D. in history, that and his shady past, which he didn't even try to conceal, brought in clientele from around the world more than eager to pay just because he had procured a piece.

Sheraton Quinn didn't do too bad either. After discovering how much cash was in the bag he had taken, he returned to Jamaica like a king. Sheraton lived well but even in Jamaica after awhile the money began to dwindle. So he brought a guitar and formed a voodoo reggae band. Now he tours the world without working, even sees his sister once a year. He brings in cash from all around the globe and stores it in the same bag he took from Macy.

All and all though, I think, Peter Winthorpe was the biggest winner. He wrote his adventures in a semi autobiographical mode which became a best seller. Recently he completed a deal for the movie rights which brought him more money at one time than he had ever made in his entire life at that point including the sales from the book. Esmerelda was happy and continued to operate the bed and breakfast while Peter hired help so he could write and still search for the dagger. He knew he might never find it but in his heart he knew it was there. Now he could say it was for history's sake and his family's stake in that glorious past.

People live and die for nothing more than ideas. History tells that story over and over. It doesn't really matter if the idea is right or wrong in the human conscious. The idea, that emotional feeling needs to be satisfied. Not the thought, the logical sense, but the feeling controls what we live for.

Whatever really happened to Jim Macy, a.k.a. Mason James, no one can really be sure. The jet ski was found near enough to Block Island that someone could have swam to shore, if the tide was right. No body was ever found and the fake dagger never showed up on the market anywhere either. There was a bizarre murder on the island about the same time that made the national newswire but it was never solved and no fingers were even pointed, at least publicly, at Jim Macy.

My personal feelings are a normal human being would have been dead before even trying to think about leaving the dock; let alone someone beat up as much as Macy with a knife hanging out of his back. Therefore, without any real proof to the contrary, I have to assume the bastard is still alive out there somewhere waiting, and no government agency is ever going to convince me otherwise.

Though as I tend to get older, I no longer feel any responsibility to save the world or even try to change it anymore. I tried that a long time ago, it didn't work then, and I'm sure it doesn't work much better now. This world ain't perfect, that's for sure. It helps creates guys like Macy when it needs them and doesn't know what to do with them when it doesn't. Luckily for the world my path is probably the only one left he is still looking to come across.

I can live with that.